ETON'S ESCAPE

Bullard's Battle
Book #3

Dale Mayer

ETON'S ESCAPE (BULLARD'S BATTLE, BOOK 3)
Dale Mayer
Valley Publishing

Copyright © 2021

ISBN-13: 978-1-773363-25-7
Print Edition

Books in This Series:

About This Book

Welcome to a new stand-alone but interconnected series from Dale Mayer. This is Bullard's story—and that of his team's. All raw, rough, incredibly capable men who have one goal: to find out who was behind the attack on their leader, before the attacker, or attackers, return to finish the job.

Stay tuned for more nonstop action as the men narrow down their suspects ... and find a way to let love back into their own empty lives.

Eton journeys to Switzerland, unimpressed at finding Garret there as his backup. Barely recovered but pissed and mobile, Garret refuses to be kept out of service any longer. Eton's intel leads them to a small village, to a woman in distress, and to someone who likes cleaning up a trail a little too much.

Living a quiet life with her aging father, Sammy is surprised by an offer of help when she gets an unexpected flat tire. Strangers in this area are not common, and neither are they well received. Still this stranger's a can-do person, and she instinctively turns to him when she soon needs additional help.

Only to find he's partly why she's in trouble—and he's got bigger troubles of his own. Now they both had to get out of this nightmare and somewhere safe and sound, ... before it's too late.

CHAPTER 1

A S SOON AS he landed in Switzerland, Eton Duram picked up a rental car but was later told to turn around and to head deeper into the countryside, hours driving time from here. Which in some ways explained why he hadn't caught a connecting flight, but also he trusted the men on his team. If they felt taking a little more convoluted route was a good idea, then it was the right thing to do. The rental vehicle was under a different name, and that was all good with him. He'd picked it up without any problem, and now, hours later, according to his phone's GPS, he was only about fifty minutes from the latest address he had been given.

As he drove away from the city onto country roads, he noted a vehicle pulled off to the side, where a woman dealt with a flat tire. He knew he needed to drive on by. He was only a few minutes away from his destination, but damn it— not even his particular brand of work should take precedence over his personal sense of humanity. Immediately another thought struck him though. What if it was a trap? Apparently a lot of people were hunting him down. The idea that she might have something to do with that just didn't sit right with him. He hit the brakes and slowly backed up. Hopping out, he walked back, every nerve on edge as he studied her.

Surprised, she turned to look at him and then shrugged. He was a stranger, probably a tourist. She tried English.

"I'm almost done," she said. "I could have used your help about twenty minutes ago though."

"How did you get the old tire off?" he asked, because the lug nuts were often very hard to loosen.

She nodded. "I had to jump on the lug wrench."

"Whatever works," he said. He took the big wrench from her hand, bent down, and gave the lug nuts on the spare a good hard turn, tightening them considerably.

"Now that I couldn't have done," she said.

Helping her pack up the lug wrench and the jack, he smiled and said, "Glad I could help."

She held out her hand. "My name is Sammy," she said. "Thank you for stopping."

"It's hard not to," he said. "Some things are just ingrained."

"Well, they didn't seem to be ingrained in the two people who went by before you," she said cheerfully. "I don't really expect much less though."

"Why is that?" he asked.

"Carjacking has become a problem here lately," she said. "People are scared."

"Are you a local?"

She nodded.

"So they would know that it's you and that you weren't likely to be carjacking them," he said, standing tall, his hands on his hips, studying the area around him. "It's a pretty rural area here, huh?"

"Not in comparison to other places," she said. "It's much more isolated out toward the ski resorts. Not that many people are in this area, but, when you get to the center of town, it really is building upon building, yet only lasts for about one-quarter mile, and then it's gone again."

He smiled at that. "Thanks for the heads-up."

"Where are you headed?"

"Some friends rented a chalet somewhere around here," he lied glibly.

"Nice," she said. "Any particular reason for choosing this part of town?"

His senses always on the alert, he shrugged and said, "Don't know. It was their choice. I just decided to come and spend a few days with them. Haven't managed to do that since my buddy got hurt."

"Ouch," she said. "I hope he's doing better."

"Better enough to get here," he said cheerfully. "I guess I'll be on my way, if you don't need any more help," he said, turning to face her.

She smiled and said, "No, I'm good. Thank you. You didn't give me your name though."

He hesitated, then flashed her a bright smile and said, "Eton."

"Eton," she said, pronouncing it slowly.

"Yes, it's a British name," he said, with a smile and a goodbye wave. He raced ahead and hopped into his vehicle, then pretended to be on his phone while he looked up her license plate. Some things were just so ingrained that he couldn't *not* do them if he tried. Next, he sent a text to Cain. **This vehicle was stopped on the road with a flat. I stopped to help her but**—He left that part hanging, and Cain replied right away.

I'm on it.

Eton started up the engine, just as she drove past him slowly. She leaned over and waved, so he smiled and waved back. Any other day he would have followed up on that lead, absolutely loving her yoga butt, slim waist, and lean body.

She was only average height, but something about her slimness made her seem taller. She also had her long blond hair in a plait down her back, and it almost reached to her butt. He had to admit it though. He really liked long hair.

In his world, it was a danger though. It could always be used as a weapon against you, but, then again, not too many women were in the type of warfare he was involved in. And Ice? Well, Ice was the exception. She'd even learned a bunch of tricks on how to get out of a hold on her hair.

Ice and Kai had worked hard on developing some self-defense moves because neither had wanted to cut their hair. And now that Ice was married and had her baby, she was looking pretty rosy and fine, indeed. Eton was glad she hadn't had to cut her hair. Something was just so very feminine about long hair. At least for him. It was always one of the first things he noticed about a woman. And, in this case, Sammy had beautiful hair. The fact that she'd been struggling with the lug nuts had also given her some bright pink cheeks and wispy hair. All in all, she was quite refreshing. Yet sadly, it was so not the right time for dating.

Shifting into Drive, he pulled back onto the country road. Following the GPS, he noted he was behind her for most of the way. As she headed into the small village that she'd described and then took a right, his turn was only two driveways past hers. Hers appeared to be more of a mainstream side road though, so he wasn't sure how far up she went. He followed the main road until he got to his turn and took it, then drove another two miles and took a left up into the hills.

As he went farther into the trees, he approved of the location. Quiet, private, easy to track from overhead, with lots of cover, in case somebody was coming after them on foot.

That was never a good thing, but it also gave them a lot of cover to go after somebody too. So it was a balance. As he rounded a corner, he saw a chalet built into the hillside. He pulled up beside the other vehicle and, grabbing his duffel bag, hopped out and headed inside.

He suspected someone would be here, and he hoped like hell it wouldn't be Garret. It was one thing to have your good friend here, but another thing completely when your good friend just got out of the hospital, after being in a coma for far too long. Eton walked to the door and knocked hard, then knocked again. When it was unlocked from the inside, he pushed it open and stepped in. Sure enough, there was Garret, a huge grin on his face. Eton dropped his bag and started swearing at him.

But instead of swearing back or having anything to say, Garret walked over and gave Eton a big hug. "Love you too, man," he said.

Eton hugged him hard, then stepped back. Looking at his buddy, he said, "Dammit, Garret. You should be back in that hospital." He wouldn't even give Garret a chance to respond. "Why the hell are you here? You should be resting."

"Any reason I can't rest here?" he asked quietly.

"You shouldn't be in the line of fire yet."

"I was in the line of fire from day one," he said. "It was me who got blown up. Remember? You think you'll pass me by on any leg of this journey? I was there with Bullard. *Bullard.* Who is still missing, in spite of the number of people we have out looking for him. Including Ice running point on that, yet we've found no sign of him. Even Terk is out there, searching the damn ethers or whatever the hell he does. No sign of Bullard. I won't sit and do nothing. I can do this. So I *will* do this. No matter if you want to send me back, I'll do this from wherever."

"I should send you back, yes," he said. "Maybe we'd get it all solved before you are physically fit and cleared to return to work again."

"I'm fit now," Garret bit off. "The rest of the team agreed, and I'm here, so you better get used to it." With that, he turned and walked away.

Grabbing his bag, Eton followed. "Well, let's hope it's a simple case of stopping by for one night and popping somebody."

"It won't be that easy," he said. "You know that."

"Do we have any information? I feel like I've been traveling forever."

"Hardly," he said. "We do have some intel, none of it terribly useful yet."

"Goddammit," he said and then swore again.

Garret grinned. "I see your mouth still spews a blue streak."

"It's a stress release," he announced and shrugged. "You've never complained before."

"I'm not complaining now," he said cheerfully. "The fact of the matter is that you care, and this is your way of showing it."

SAMMY HEDRICK DROVE home slowly. It had been an opportune time to have the stranger stop and ask if she needed help. Too bad he hadn't shown up a little earlier. But, if he had, he would have seen the slashed tire. She still wasn't sure why the tire hadn't given up the ghost a whole lot earlier. But she'd only left her friend's house a few minutes ago, and she had yet to tell her dad what had happened. He would be pretty pissed off and upset to think that she'd somehow gotten a flat tire at her friend's place. Sammy wasn't exactly sure that it had happened there. She was hoping to have her dad check it out. But it depended on how he was doing first, sick or not sick. Most of the time he was sick these days. There just wasn't any break at all.

As she drove through town, she saw the stranger behind her.

Eton was his name. She rolled that around in her mind. Wasn't there a university or something called that? Oh, yeah. Eton College somewhere in England? He didn't really look English though. She wasn't sure what he was. Big, that was one thing, and tall. Well tanned and used to a tough physical life, judging by the muscles. He was a male in his prime. And she heartily approved.

The fact that she'd been taken in by his sex appeal was something she chalked up to the fact that she'd been on a bit of a dry spell. As Annie would say, a very long dry spell. But Sammy had had enough short-term relationships that had gone nowhere that she really wasn't interested in taking that route anymore.

She wanted something that would last. Something that was steadfast as compared to her previous relationships. It wasn't like the guys were the problem either. She had come across as *too intense*, according to one of them. Another said he wasn't ready for a commitment, while she obviously was. The first one though, that was just weird. He'd been there, and then he'd been gone. She thought the term *ghosting* applied in his case. She suspected he'd be back, and, sure enough, a couple months later he'd turned up, sending her a little smiley emoji saying, *Hook up?* She hadn't even responded.

The last thing she needed was to always be waiting on some guy to get in touch with her. She had better things to do with her time. Now that she had finished her architectural degree, she had to make some big decisions. She could go to a big city and set up her own business. But who would hire her with so little experience, since she was only twentynine? It was a good thing that her father was also an architect. A fairly major architect. He was famous for his underground homes and his Swiss house.

She absolutely loved him and wanted him to keep on with his work. The trouble was that his work was starting to drag, right along with his health. He had asked her to come work for him, and she'd been his assistant for years now, while attending university part-time, but it didn't feel quite right to step in as his replacement. If he could hold on for another four or five years, she could make a name for herself, apart from his reputation, at the same time. In the meantime, not so much.

She parked outside her home, her father's famous house, hopped out, and wondered what she should do about the tire. Deciding there was no point in keeping it in her trunk, she should bring it closer to the house for her father to inspect. She opened up the back of the car, struggled to get it from the vehicle, then rolled it up to the side of the house and just plunked it down. It had a decent-size slash. At least it wasn't like somebody had taken a knife and jammed it in a bunch of times, like some psycho ex-lover, but somebody had stabbed it once and then definitely cut it.

Of course it could have come from something off the driveway or along the road, but still it didn't seem likely. Frowning, she headed inside. "Dad, I'm home," she said, calling out for him.

She headed into the kitchen, put on the teakettle, and threw down her purse. Obviously it said something about how rattled she was that the tea came first. Then she went looking for her father. He was in his second-floor office, still at the drafting board, but staring out the window, an almost vacant smile on his face. She rushed to his side. "Dad, how are you doing?" she asked gently.

He looked up at her, gave a mental shake, and smiled. "I'm fine," he said, with more force than necessary. She frowned at him. He smiled, reached over, and patted her hand. "Honest."

"Well, I'm back from Annie's," she said, "and I've put on the teakettle."

He pushed his chair back with a big smile. "A piece of that spice cake would be lovely," he said. "A cup of tea and cake—the elixirs of God."

"We need to do something about lunch before cake," she teased.

He frowned. "I'm not very hungry," he admitted.

Her heart sank again. He was never hungry anymore, and eating was something she had to force him to do. "I'll go make you anything you want," she promised. "What would you like?" He just stared at her, and she knew that some of his thoughts were already drifting away. "Never mind," she said. "I'll make something, and you can have it before cake."

At that, he smiled and said, "Cake sounds good." Then he returned to his work.

She stepped up behind him to look down at the work he had done. One of the odd things about his condition was that his mental clarity seemed to be sharp when he was working. At the end of every day, she came and checked over his work to ensure everything was solid and wouldn't collapse under the intrusion of the real world. She patted him gently on the shoulder, as he brought out his ruler again and started marking line blinds, involved in piping systems. "How is the job going?"

"Almost done," he said cheerfully. "Two more to do after this."

She looked at the stack of files and frowned. "I think it's more than that," she said worriedly.

"I'll only deal with two ahead at a time," he said.

She laughed and said, "Okay, we'll do it your way."

"I'll need your help on this one though later," he said.

"Sure enough, after lunch," she said. "Unless you need my help now?" She stopped to look at him.

He shook his head. "I'll just finish this section here," he said. "Then, after lunch, I'll get your help."

She nodded and headed downstairs. Back in the kitchen she opened up the fridge, wondering what she would feed him. Not only did he have no appetite but his stomach was touchy too. The doctors had run a lot of tests, but he wasn't exactly forthcoming with the results. That bothered her too. It was just the two of them. She wasn't at all sure what she would do if and when he passed in the not-so-distant future. That was something she didn't dare think about.

Resolutely she pulled out the ingredients for an omelet. If nothing else, he generally would eat eggs.

CHAPTER 2

A FTER HER FATHER had eaten, Sammy went back up to the office with him, where she sat down at his side, and the two of them worked on the current project. She knew the projects would bother him, if they stuck around too long. The designs were great and had been sent off, came back with changes, were fixed and sent off again, and it was an ongoing process. And the one that he was currently working on was particularly troubling. He had stopped taking new orders because, as he said, he was backed up. And he was.

She just hoped beyond hope that maybe they could get through the whole stack before he left her behind. By the time late afternoon hit, she looked up at the wall clock—four-thirty already. "Wow," she said, "we did well today." She looked over, and her father was in the recliner, snoozing gently. She sighed, got up, grabbed a blanket, and threw it over him. She leaned over, gave him a kiss on the cheek, and said, "I'll go see what we are doing about dinner," she murmured. He, of course, gave no response.

She walked back to the desk, shut down the task lights, carefully rolled up the blueprints, set them off to the side so they were safe, and then headed downstairs. Once out of the office, her mind immediately went back to the tire, and she wondered just what she was supposed to do about that. She could call the shop to get it fixed, but, in the meantime, she didn't have a spare; so, if something else happened, she'd be stuck on the road. That, of course, brought her mind around to the tall, dark Eton. "No," she said to herself, laughing, "he's a tall blondie." But that *tall, dark, and handsome* thing rolled around in her mind because it fit in every other aspect.

Giving her head a shake, she went to the kitchen and pulled out chicken and made a light stir-fry for her father. The doctors, what little they'd told her, said that his nutritional needs were not being met because he wasn't eating, and to make sure he ate lots of vegetables. By the time dinner was cooked, she set it on the dining room table, two plates with lids on top, and went to get her father. She was halfway up the stairs when she heard him call down, "I'm coming. I'm coming."

She smiled and said, "Good. It's all served up and ready."

"You can call me before you serve, you know," he said in exasperation.

"Oh, quit your grumping. As usual I always like to have it dished up and ready for you," she said, with a chuckle. Really, it was her secret strategy to get him to eat more. Left to dish up for himself, he barely took any food at all.

They sat down at the dining room table, staring out over the view. "I love this house," he said contentedly.

"Me too," she said, as she reached over and patted his hand.

"It will be yours one day," he said, then added, "soon," a word that made her heart break.

"Well, hopefully not for a few more years," she said lightly, not wanting him to get into that conversation.

"Maybe," he said, "but you know we've been offered a

decent price for it."

Her heart froze, and she stared at him in shock. "Are you thinking about selling?"

He immediately gave a headshake. "No, not at all," he said. "I want to be here right to the end."

She let that one slip past her too, because to open up a discussion about that would just bring up what he saw as his impending death. "Besides, it doesn't matter how good an offer it is," she said. "This is your home. And it's not like you need the money."

"Isn't that amazing?" he said, with a chuckle. "I hope you make it as big as I did."

"I hope so too," she said.

"What will you do … after?"

She swallowed hard. "I don't know," she said. "I can't even begin to think about that. I won't. I don't want to be without you, Dad."

"I know, sweetie." He reached over, linked his fingers with hers, and said, "But it'll happen."

She nodded. "It will, but it doesn't have to be today or tomorrow."

"Understood," he said, with a smile.

"Come on now. Let's eat." She turned the conversation to other topics, chattering as they ate to keep him distracted. Finally she looked at the kitchen and said, "Well, that was tasty. But I need to clean up."

"Sounds good," he said. "Is there any more of that cake?"

She laughed. "Absolutely."

"Well, I'll go sit in the other room," he said. "Tea and cake—that sounds perfect."

And, with his mind once again set on that cake and his

tea, she watched as he slowly made his way from the dining room. Every step looked painful. She sighed, turned on the teakettle, and proceeded to wash the dishes. As much as her heart didn't want to face it, she knew that the day was coming, and it was coming very quickly. She didn't know what she would do when she lost him. It was just too heartbreaking to consider.

IT DIDN'T TAKE long to get Eton installed in the small chalet, particularly since Garret had arrived here a good eight hours ahead of Eton and already had the electronics set up.

"Okay, so what did I miss?" Eton asked, shaking off the stiffness from his travels in the car.

"What did *you* miss? God, getting caught up with the news after I woke up and got my wits about me, now that was an adventure," Garret said, smiling wryly. "This will be a piece of cake, especially since there isn't much to tell."

"That must have been a trip. One minute you're in a plane, and, the next thing you know, you wake up in the hospital, and they tell you how you've crashed at sea, floated around on wreckage with Ryland, got rescued by a hot girl, nearly drowned in a storm, and had been in a coma ever since."

"Worse yet, while I was unconscious, Ryland somehow got the girl to fall for him. What the hell?"

"So I heard. Wait until you see Cain though. Ryland's not the only one."

"What? No way."

Eton nodded. "Seriously, man, it's really great to see you still standing. Let's get to it. So you've got a little information but not a whole lot, is that what I'm hearing?"

"We traced Tristan's particularly interesting cell phone calls to two towns from here," Garret said. "And, yeah, we could have set up closer, but we're already pretty conspicuous as it is. Plus these hills here behind us," he said, "they back onto the other town."

At that, Eton smiled and said, "So we just go up the hill, and we should have a pretty decent signal to track?"

"Yes," he said. "We also don't have any guarantee that the person connected to Tristan is still there."

"But you got something?"

"Absolutely. Tracked over several days and weeks. That's how far we've managed to go back."

"Okay, so he is staying there—or at least had been, up until Tristan's death."

"Exactly."

Eton had already brought Garret up to snuff on what had happened in Sicily. And now they were tracking down the rest of the numbers on Tristan's phone. "Any luck on the driver who pulled away after shooting Tristan?"

"His truck was found a few miles away in a ditch," Garret said. "It was a rental, rented by Tristan, under Tristan's real name."

"But not likely rented by him, I suppose?"

"Could have been, or they could have just set up that rental vehicle like that, knowing it would be a getaway car."

"And nothing on the ballistics, correct?"

"No, nothing on the ballistics."

"God, what a mess there," Eton said.

"Yeah, your face is still showing some of the damage."

He smiled and said, "Just a sign of my close encounter with Tristan."

"One side is a little puffy."

He grinned at that.

"What was that happy look about?"

"Oh, I met a woman on the way here," he said. "She didn't appear to notice."

"Right, I checked that out, from the license plate number you sent. Sammy something." He quickly brought up what he knew. "No arrest record, so I dug deeper. Architecture degree and is currently working for her father. He's a famous architect. Both have been really close."

"So he lives here locally?"

"Yes," Garret replied and pointed. "It's basically a twenty-minute walk in that direction."

"Nice," Eton said, with a light whistle.

"What? Did she interest you?"

"She was pretty fine," he said, "but, more than that, she was a doer. Instead of waiting for help, she already had the spare tire on."

"Did she say what happened, how she got the flat?"

"No, and I didn't ask. The tire was already loaded before I got there."

"Wow," he said. "Won't see too many women doing that."

"Not in this world of cell phones and roadside service, no," he said, "but it was all good."

"Uh-oh."

There must have been something in Eton's tone of voice because Garret was grinning at him. "Yeah, not happening," Eton said. "I don't need anything taking me away from this job."

"Oh, Cain doesn't feel like what he ended up with took him away from his job."

Eton changed the topic. "Enough. Now back to the cell

phone signals. Where does it trace back to? A house or something?"

"The property has multiple buildings on it."

"Dang," Eton replied. "So it's not like it points to one single person and says, 'This is the guy.'"

"Not only that, it looks like it's a company."

"As in?"

"Bands Securities."

"Bands? I didn't think that security company was in Switzerland."

"Yes, I know," Garret said. "Bottom line is that apparently twelve people work there."

"So, either this entire location of the company is involved, or some individual is using it as a base."

"Or a visitor or a delivery person? There could be a bunch of other explanations, including somebody who does contract work," Garret pointed out.

"Right, so a simple search won't necessarily give us all the right answers."

"Well, I've just pulled up a list of all the full-time employees," he said. He printed it out and handed it to Eton. "These are just the ones here."

"Bands has other branches, right?"

"Yes, closest one is in Berlin," he said.

"Right, so it could also be somebody who came back and forth from the other office as well."

"Exactly." Garret hesitated but looked at him. "We can't count out the fact that it could also be spouses."

"No, we sure can't," Eton said. "Okay, do we have any other lists? You take one, and I take another?"

"Unless he is a staffer there. All of them are part-time," he said, "so the staff list for this town is much longer."

"Let me start with that one," Eton said, reaching across for his list. "And you take the permanent employees, who I suppose are the managers and such."

Garret nodded and found his list to check.

At that, they sat down to research the people involved. After about an hour, Eton broke the silence. "First four of mine have raised no flags," Eton said. "This fifth one though—"

"What?"

"Well, he drives a Mercedes, a sports model at that. I would really like to know what his salary is and whether he can legitimately afford it," Eton said.

"If he's young, it doesn't mean he can afford it, you know. Just that he really wanted it."

The way Garret said it was so dry that Eton had to laugh. "True enough." But Eton put an asterisk beside that name and kept on going.

After a few more minutes Garret sat back. "Not much here."

"I've finished mine," Eton said, "and the only one who flashed at all is the one I mentioned earlier."

"Well, guess you better hack into the company and seek out his paycheck."

"Can get that off his credit reports faster maybe," Eton noted.

He started working his way through the information databases they could access easily. When that didn't give him anything, he went to the guy's bank account. Something supposedly not easy to accomplish, but, for them, it was fairly simple. Terrifying to think of all the people not aware of this, as Eton and others moved around in their finances behind their backs. The general population felt secure in their annual subscriptions for security software, said to prevent identify theft or to prevent hackers from access to their information. Little did they know that Eton and men like him all around the world weren't deterred at all.

In moments, he had located the man's bank account and found not a hell of a lot of money. In fact, a large part of his paycheck went to cover the monthly loan payment on that sports car. "Idiot," Eton muttered under his breath.

"Knew it. Was I right, or was I right?" Garret said, laughing.

"You were right," he said. "Jesus, the things these guys think are important. That kills me."

"He's probably young and trolling for chicks with it," he said.

"God, whatever. How about your list? Anything?"

"Only one of interest to me," he said. "The boss has been married three times, so the alimony payments are killing him. His house is mortgaged to the hilt, and his car is leased, probably because the last one was about to get repossessed, so he surrendered it."

"So his financial pressures make him susceptible to bribes, payouts, and blackmail."

"All of the above and more," Garret said, nodding. "You know what? It seems they've always been one step ahead of us. It wouldn't surprise me if they had another party in place here as well."

"Yeah, they've always got another hand to play. At some point soon," he said, "we have to get closer." Eton stood to stretch.

"No doubt, and it could be anyone really."

"No kidding. After what we found in Sicily, it's shocking to think what people would do for a little bit of money."

"Right, those people were something, weren't they?"

He just shook his head. "I feel bad for Petra," Eton said.

"I do too. She just lost her father and her sister, and now her aunt and uncle are being charged with multiple offenses, many of them against her. That's pretty sick," Garret said. "At least she's financially stable though, so that's one good thing."

"Yeah, but that's what made her a target in the first place. No doubt she'd rather have her father." Eton paced the room. "*Money.* It's so easy to look at anybody and think they are involved somehow. If they have money, or if they don't, we assume they are guilty of something."

"It's the job. It makes us jaded."

Eton chuckled. "Petra kept pointing that out. Cain's got his hands full with that one." Returning his attention to the list, Eton frowned. "We need to broaden this, maybe start with the spouses and other family members," Eton said.

"Yeah, I was hoping we wouldn't have to, but we might as well. At least if we don't find anything interesting, we will have cleared it." They quickly started with the names of anybody attached to an employee who was over eighteen. When Eton came to the punk with the sports car, he realized the kid had no steady girlfriend, but his parents were wealthy. "This punkhead with the car is just trying to keep up appearances," Eton said. "His parents have money."

"He probably crashed every car his parents ever gave him, so they cut him off and told him to go get his own."

Eton laughed at that. "Unfortunately that's all too possible, and having to drive what he could afford was too much for his ego." Heading to the motor vehicles and insurances databases for Switzerland, Eton quickly confirmed that Garret was correct. "You are almost magical," he said jokingly. "You nailed it."

"Nah, just basic young-man mentality."

"Well, I need to get past the young-man mentality and get into something much darker."

"Don't write him off though," Garret said, looking at him. "If you think about it, he has a lot of reasons to do something for money."

"True, and showing up every day to earn a regular paycheck probably isn't his style."

On a hunch, Eton buckled down and hacked into the security company and checked the personnel records. "Not only are his wages only average but he'd been written up several times for insubordination and insolence. I'll have to run some of this through a translator to be sure, but it looks to me like he's even had his pay docked several times."

"Which all makes him pretty high up in my mind," Garret said. "Want me to check out the parents?" Eton nodded and read off their names. Garret set to work and soon had a start. "Well, the parents used to work for the military."

"Both of them?"

"Yes, in the Swiss military."

"Well, I suppose the Swiss guards could have their bad apples, like everybody else," Eton said. "Though it doesn't mean that they are of the same ilk as these lowlife bastards who are after us."

"No, doesn't look like it. Several commendations are in both files for good behavior. Several awards as well."

"Complete opposite of their son then. Everything I find makes it appear that he's an only child and that they've doted on him since birth. Looks like they'd finally had enough with that last crash."

"Why is it that parents can't handle their kids?" Garret

said. "Somebody's got to do it."

At that, Eton let out a bark of laughter and started digging into the rest of them on his list. He shoved his laptop away two hours later and said, "I didn't find anything much, did you?"

"Well, I'm still working on the boss."

"Why is that?"

"Wife number two, she skated on blackmail charges."

"What?" Eton sighed, leaned back, and looked at Garret; then he reached for his laptop. "What's her name?" With that, he quickly entered the name Garret provided. Marielle had been wife number two for a whole fourteen months. "Who was she blackmailing?"

"The boss who became her hubby."

"He turned her in?"

"Yes, and charges were filed, but he dropped all the charges because he didn't want to go to trial. He bought her off instead."

"He bought her off? How is that fair?"

"The reason for the divorce was because he was flirting around."

"Wow," Eton said, chuckling. "So, chances are it's not related to this?"

"I highly doubt it, but I'll pursue it a little further," Garret replied. Frowning, he pushed his chair back, shook his head, and said, "Outside of that, I've got nothing."

"So, we've got a boss mortgaged to the hilt with ex-wife troubles, and we've got a twenty-three-year-old kid trying to live beyond his means. Other than that, nothing's popping," Eton said, scratching his head.

"But that's just a start," Garret said.

Eton nodded. "Did you shop for food?"

"Yeah, the fridge is full," he replied. "I took steaks out for dinner."

At that, Eton's stomach sang out, and he said, "Hallelujah! I think I can smell those grilled steaks already." He walked into the kitchen, took one look at the steaks marinating, and sniffed the air. "They look good. What did you use, a garlic marinade?"

"Yep," he said, "salt and a garlic spray. Not too fancy." Garret looked at him. "I guess you didn't eat much the last couple days, did you?"

"No. Not much at all. Just as needed."

"We'll fix that here," he said. "I figured, after we eat, we should do a night trip over the hill."

"Works for me," Eton said.

Garret grabbed potatoes and asked, "How soon do you want to eat?"

"An hour's good, but thirty minutes is better." Eton looked at the potatoes, frowned, and said, "Those are gonna take a bit, if you're thinking baked."

"I'll grate them," Garret said. He quickly grabbed two big ones and found a grater in the cupboard. "By the time you've got these steaks done, we'll have potatoes too."

"Are you planning on veggies or just starch and protein?" Eton joked, as he walked toward him. "How about a salad?"

"We can do that."

Eton pulled out salad fixings, then went outside and lit the barbecue pit. When he came back, Garret already had the grated potatoes in a hot pan. "You just put them right in the pan?"

"If I had time, I'd put them in a bowl and let the starch collect, then rinse them off," Garret said, "but we don't have time." He put the two big potatoes, now grated, in thin layers in two hot pans with a drizzle of olive oil, then seasoned them and just let them cook. While they were browning, Eton took the steaks outside and tossed them on the barbecue pit, while Garret laid out the salad.

As they sat down to a hot dinner little more than a scant eight minutes later, Eton took his first bite of steak and smiled. "Now my stomach won't kill me," he said. Laughing together, they each enjoyed their dinner, as they discussed their plans. "On a hill like this, when the sun goes down, you're pretty well hitting dusk. We're at seven-thirty right now," Eton said.

Garret nodded. "So I figure we should hit the road by eight. We'll probably have a ten-minute hike to the top of the hill. We've got some equipment that I want to set out to see if we can get any better tracking on that cell phone."

"We need that phone turned on in order to track it."

"Yeah, but most people just leave them on these days."

"True, unless they are one-way burners," Eton said. Dishes washed, they quickly gathered up the gear they needed, and, with a quick look around, Eton asked, "Have you got something in place in the event we get an unwanted visitor?"

"All set up," Garret said cheerfully.

Eton glanced at him. "Jeez, you aren't taking any chances on me getting pissed off and sending you home, huh?"

"Not a chance of that happening." Garret shot him a hard look. "You're here. I'm here," he said. "They've taken one shot at me. I know what these guys can do."

"And I can look after myself." Eton brushed off his concerns. He knew what Garret would do with that too.

"Don't be an ass," he said. "The fact that you can handle it alone doesn't matter. I'll be here anyway."

"Got it," he said, and the two of them headed up the mountain.

CHAPTER 3

AFTER HER DAD had settled in front of the TV, Sammy looked at him and said, "Dad, I'm going for a run."

He looked up, smiled faintly, and said, "That's a good idea, dear."

She hesitated, since she really didn't like leaving him. But she'd become a bit of a cross-country runner as a way to relieve the stress in her life that had grown with the progression of his debilitating condition. She quickly changed into running pants, a tank top, and her running shoes. It was later than normal, but she still loved to run in the dark. She knew the paths up and around the hills like the back of her hand. She picked up her water bottle, tightened her fitness watch, and headed out the kitchen door.

The only problem with her route was that it was uphill to begin with, so she didn't get much chance to warm up and to stretch. Typically she would do it before she left, but, with the stress from the flat tire and the worry about her father, everything was coiled inside her, and she just had to get out and to let loose.

She raced sideways up the hill, not letting herself stop, even as she gasped for breath, settling into a long easy recovery jog. She wasn't sure exactly what weather was in the forecast; she hadn't even checked. But the stars were out, so it was bright enough for a nice long run. She wouldn't do too much, just enough to hit that point where she could feel all the stress inside crumbling away. That was always a moment of sheer joy.

However, right now, she felt she was running on rubber bands instead of feet, those bands kicking her legs faster and faster. When one of her feet came back, when she felt more grounded, it told her, *more and more.* By the time she'd done forty-five minutes, zigzagging her way back and forth to the top of the incline, she stopped, her hands on her hips, and took several slow deep breaths. She couldn't afford to stand here for long, but she could at least rest for a bit. Hearing a voice behind her, she spun and almost fell over in the dark. "Who's there?" she asked.

In a surprise move, the stranger from the road stepped forward.

She looked at him. "Eton?"

"Hi, Sammy," he said, with that lopsided grin.

In the dark, he looked a little more intimidating than he had on the road. Instinctively she took a step back.

He immediately put up both hands. "You're okay," he said. "I'm not gonna hurt you."

"Well, that's good," she said, "because I've been running for the last forty-five minutes. I'm not sure I have too much left to fight with."

"You've been running in the dark up in these hills?" Another man appeared at Eton's side.

She studied him, but it was hard to see his features. But there was something about him, that same strong presence and power that Eton had. These were men who were capable of doing shit. She nodded slowly. "Yes. I often do it at the end of the day, just as a way to release some stress."

"Right," he said. "That's a hell of a way to do it, if you're running up the hills cross-country."

"Today was a particularly stressful day," she said.

"The tire?" Eton's tone was sharp.

She shrugged. "It's just so random. No reason for it," she said. "It's looked like somebody stabbed a knife into it." When she saw both men go still, she felt all the more nervous.

"Got any enemies around?"

"None who would have done that," she murmured. Eyeing the two of them, she continued, "Unless it was you two."

"We are not your enemies," Eton said. "And I stopped to help. Remember?"

"I know. I'm sorry," she said. She took a deep breath, looked at the way she'd come up, and said, "Guess I'll head back down now."

"Are you sure you should be out here running at night?" Eton asked.

"I always have," she said. "I've never given it a thought. Why?"

"Well, it's just that looking into things, like slashed tires, is the kind of work we do," Eton said. "Sort of anyway."

"So you're in law enforcement?"

"Let's call it more of a *global* law enforcement," he said, with that same half grin again.

"As long as you are not a mercenary," she said, taking another step back, totally unsure how to feel about him. Everything he said sounded right, but, at the same time, he was a stranger, and she didn't know if it was safe to trust him or not.

"We aren't here to hurt you," he reiterated. "I'm just concerned. If your tire was deliberately cut or slashed, generally that means somebody was either hoping to come upon you, broken down along the road, or worse—that you might have had an accident. Are you sure you don't have someone in your world with a reason for any of that? Or even transients or local ruffians?"

"I was visiting a friend of mine," she said. "She lives alone, and I figure my tire was cut there, but I didn't realize it until I was on the road and felt the wobble and the pull on my steering wheel."

"How long were you there? And is her car okay?" the other man asked.

"Just a couple hours," she said. "I stopped there and had a cup of coffee with her, and then I headed straight home to make sure my dad got some lunch. I haven't talked to my friend, so I don't know about her car." At that, her voice almost broke.

"Your dad? Is he okay?"

She shook her head. "I shouldn't even be telling you this, but his condition is declining. Mentally and physically. I don't think he has too much longer, and, honestly, watching the process is hard. Really hard." Instantly she could feel the sympathy emanating from both men.

She just shook her head, wiped her hands on her running pants, and said, "I've got to go." Then she bolted down the same pathway that she had run up, and her heart slammed against her chest the whole way. If something were going on with these two men, she'd basically just told them that she lived alone with nobody to help look after her. She should have given the impression that she lived with a huge strong and jealous boyfriend, not an aging and sickly father. But still she couldn't find any reason for her openness, beyond the fact that she really liked the little bit of Eton she'd seen, and he inspired confidence. She just wasn't sure how the hell that worked.

"THAT'S SAMMY?" GARRET asked.

Eton nodded.

"Love her accent. I guess the Swiss accommodate visitors by speaking English as well."

Again Eton nodded, with a one-armed shrug.

Garret whistled. "Well, I can see the attraction," he said. "And she is superfit."

"Absolutely," he said, "but I had no idea she was into cross-country running."

"And in the dark."

"I used to do that myself," Eton said. "It feels very different from the normal cross-country running during the day."

"If you say so. She looked like she was enjoying herself," Garret said smoothly, "until we came along anyway."

"It's odd though," he said. "If it were me running, I wouldn't give it a thought. But because she is out here running, I really want to go after her and make sure she gets home safe."

"That would probably just confirm her worry that you are a stalker—or worse," Garret joked.

Eton winced at that. "She definitely didn't look all that happy to see me."

"Well, she didn't ask, and it's probably smart of her, but here we are, at the top of the mountain. Plus, although she didn't see it, the equipment we've got would hardly inspire confidence."

"No, you're right," he said. "I wish I knew where she lived though, so I could go by in the morning and reassure her that we weren't up to anything sketchy."

"But we are though," Garret said. "And she is a good reminder that we are not alone."

At that, Eton turned around, nodded, and said, "We still haven't picked up any signal."

"I know. I'm wondering if the guy has a second phone and keeps this one off, unless he needs to make a call."

"That would be about our luck," he said. "So let's finish setting up the equipment, and then we'll leave it here," he said, "but I also want to run a transmitter down to the house."

"It won't be a quick trip up here," Garret warned.

"I know, but, if we can trigger something on the phone, we could come up and see if we can get a location. The other thing is," he said, "we should put Ice on this."

"I already tried that, and she's working on it, but we're here in place," he said. "So the chances of her getting a better location on our target's cell phone aren't likely."

Just then the machinery in front of them made a weird clicking sound.

"Interesting," Garret said, jumping over to the equipment. "Looks like the phone just turned on."

"Location?" Eton asked. He stared down at the village on the other side of the hill. "It's not very busy down there, is it?"

"No, only about five thousand live on that side, and then around forty-five hundred are on this side."

"So this is Switzerland in this area, huh? These little dotted communities?"

"Yeah, but they are all close enough to get into the city, if they need to, for commuting."

"So, they're like little bedroom communities."

"Exactly," said Garret. "Unless any businesses are around that would support this number of residents, I would suspect that almost every one of these households has at least one person who commutes."

"That would suck," Eton said. "I hate commuting as it is. On a daily basis, that would really finish me."

"Well, aren't you the lazy ass," Garret said. As he bent to study the equipment, he said, "Look. A call is being made right now." He transmitted the data to his phone. "And it's coming from the village, from the far side up on that hill that we can see in the distance."

Sure enough, Eton saw a hill, if you could call it that. It certainly wasn't a mountain, and it was barely above ground level, as far as Eton was concerned, but he saw lights dancing between the trees of various houses. "Okay, I should go down and head that way in the vehicle," he muttered.

"We should have done that from the beginning. I just didn't think we would get this lucky on the first try," Garret said.

"I'm already on my way," Eton said. "Keep an eye on that. I'll be in the vehicle and heading down the road in, like, six minutes."

"You would have been faster if you were chasing after her."

"Yeah, and scared her to death too," he said and headed down the hillside toward the car.

CHAPTER 4

SAMMY GOT BACK home, out of breath. Instead of that sense of release and peace rushing over her, it was as if something else had curled up inside. Why hadn't she thought to ask what were they doing up there at night? Something about the nighttime activities, especially when the men were dressed all in black, gave her the heebie-jeebies about what criminal acts they might be up to. He said that they were working in the world, doing stuff that caught bad guys; yet he denied being in law enforcement. So just what the hell was it that they were doing? She hated to even think about it, but, now that the idea had surfaced, she couldn't let it go. That's all she thought about.

As she walked inside, her body slick with sweat, her father looked up from the television, his gaze lucid and clear. "Well, don't you look like you had a lovely run?"

She smiled at him and said, "I did. I'll go have a shower now though, okay?"

He just nodded.

As she headed to the shower, she remembered the men asking about whether Annie's car had been damaged as well. On a whim, Sammy texted her friend and asked if her vehicle's tires were okay. Then she headed into the shower. As she was drying off, she heard her phone ringing. She picked it up to see Annie had tried twice already. When

Sammy called her back, Annie answered right away.

"How did you know?"

"It just occurred to me that, if somebody had deliberately slashed my tire, then potentially they had also taken out yours."

"Well, now I feel really terrified," she said.

"Why?"

"Because my tires were also slashed, and I can't go anywhere now."

"You've got your home security system. Make sure to turn it on."

"It is," she said, "but remember. I couldn't afford the full package, so I just got the basic coverage."

"Right," she said. "Thinking about that, you've never had any trouble before though, have you?"

"No, but I've never had my tires slashed either," Annie said bitterly.

"Any idea who might do this?"

"I was thinking my ex," she admitted. "You know how he is. He scares me sometimes."

"True, but you haven't had any contact with Jorge in weeks, have you?"

Annie hesitated and then said, "I didn't tell you, but he got the divorce papers I sent him."

"No, you didn't tell me about that," she said. "Damn."

"I know, and, although I'm driving the vehicle, don't forget it was ours. And now I own the car, and I get to stay in this rental."

"Did you get a response on the divorce papers being served? Like, did he contact your lawyer at all?"

"No, not at all," Annie said, "unless you want to take the tires as a response."

"Were you ever in danger with him while married, even dating beforehand?" Sammy asked, with some urgency.

"You mean, did he ever beat me? No, he was rudely abusive, but he never hit me," she said. "So I highly doubt that he would do that right now. But it's also possible that something else is going on here and that the divorce has triggered violence that was undetected all that time."

"And now you're making me feel like shit," she said. "I shouldn't have texted you at nighttime."

"No, you shouldn't have," she said, "because now I won't sleep at all." And, with that, Annie hung up.

Sammy got dressed in her pajamas, grabbed her robe, and went downstairs. "You up for some hot chocolate, Dad?"

But, as she looked at her father in the den for an answer, he was sleeping gently in place. She walked over to the teakettle and put it on, and, through the kitchen window, she saw headlights from a car driving down from the houses up on the hillside. She guessed that maybe one of those houses was where Eton and his friend came from. She knew of one chalet out there that was often leased or rented out to visitors.

As she watched the twin beams, the vehicle took off past her own lone road and driveway, and all she could think of was, *Where was it going at this time of night?*

Then her phone rang again. It was Annie. "Can I come stay with you?"

"Yes, of course," she said, her mind flipping immediately to whether the spare room bedding was clean and ready to go. "I didn't mean to scare you earlier."

"Too late," she said. And then she stopped. "But I can't come to you," she added, "because I don't have wheels."

"I'll come and pick you up," Sammy said immediately.

"I'm on my way," she said, hanging up. She looked down at her pajamas, shrugged, turned the teakettle off, and walked back into her bedroom, where she quickly changed into a pair of leggings and a running tank. And she walked down the front steps and got into her vehicle, wondering where her keys were. *In my hand.* "Dammit," she said, "now I can't even think straight for worry."

She tossed the phone on the seat beside her and turned on the engine and headed down the driveway to the main road. It wasn't necessarily her driveway, but it was a small gravel road that four or five of them used and that connected to the main road. As soon as she turned onto it, her thoughts went to the vehicle ahead of her. It was long gone and out of sight, but still she couldn't help by wonder. Was it Eton? And, if so, what was he up to? As she pulled in, she found Annie standing on the front porch, with a carry-on bag.

She raced to the car, opened it up, and hopped in. She was literally shivering.

"What happened?" Sammy asked.

Annie held out her phone and said, "This." Then she tapped the surface, so Sammy saw the message underneath. It was a text message. **Bitch, you won't get away with this.**

"Oh, shit," Sammy said, shaking her head. "Did you send that to the lawyer?"

"I should have, shouldn't I?" She quickly forwarded the message on to her attorney. "I don't know whether it's my ex," she said, "but I don't know who else it could have been."

"You can't jump to conclusions either," Sammy said, "but that also doesn't mean that he's not already on his way here to take you out."

"No, but most of the time, it's too late for the woman to do anything, and the cops always say they can't do anything until something happens."

Sammy knew that all too well, having her own knowledge of a few cases around the world with similar issues of domestic violence. "Well, you're coming back to stay with me tonight. Then tomorrow, in the light of day, we'll figure out what to do. And you need to tell your lawyer that your tires were slashed too."

"Right."

While her friend's fingers were busy, Sammy turned the car around, headed back to the main road, and then took the turn on up to her house. As she walked into the house with Annie at her side, Annie said quietly, "I forgot to ask. Will your dad mind?"

Sammy shook her head. "No," she said, "and chances are he won't even realize you're here until morning."

As it was, the guest bedroom was on the bottom floor, with the other bedrooms all on the second floor. Sammy settled her friend in and said, "I was just about to make hot chocolate when you called me."

"That would be perfect," Annie said, tossing her bag on the floor and taking off her sweater. "I'll come with you."

As they went into the kitchen, Sammy looked out the window and could swear somebody was in the trees, watching them. She froze, took a step toward the window, and the shadow broke its form and took off down the driveway. Only she saw it long enough to realize that it really was a man, before he disappeared into the tree line.

"What's the matter?" Annie asked.

She looked at her friend, thought about the possible answers to give, smiled, and said, "I thought I saw a deer."

"Deer are everywhere up here," she said, with a wave of her hand.

Only it wasn't a deer. It was something much more sinister. And that terrified Sammy. As she walked into the den, her dad still slept on the couch. Annie had followed along, then stopped and smiled, a soft look on her face. "I have such good memories of time spent here."

"Me too," Sammy said. "The time is going by faster than I'd like."

"I know," she said, "and there is no way to stop it."

"More the reason," she said, "to make the best of the time we have." Back in the kitchen, she put on the teakettle and, while they were waiting for it to boil, she went out to the living room and stood close to the curtain, checking to see if she could see anyone. But there was nothing.

Annie joined her and, in a low whisper, said, "You still going to tell me that you thought you saw a deer?"

She looked at her friend, frowned, and said, "You've got enough to worry about."

"True, but I don't like things being kept from me," she warned.

"I thought I saw a man in the trees," Sammy said, "and he went down that direction."

Annie looked at her in horror and stared outside. "I can't see anything," she complained.

"No," she said, "and neither can I. For all I know, it was just my imagination."

"But, after the tires, you are not so sure, are you?"

The accusation in her friend's voice stiffened her back, and Sammy looked at her, smiled, and said, "But even if it was a man," she said, "that doesn't mean he is doing anything but walking up and down this road. Don't forget it connects multiple houses."

"Well, that's true," Annie said, taking another look. "It

could be somebody renting or visiting anybody around here. I don't know why everybody always wears black, when they are outside at night though," she snapped.

"I know. I feel the same way," she said.

"I'm surprised. You mentioned you fixed your tire yourself."

"I did most of it myself, but a guy stopped and helped me tighten up the lug nuts, after I'd gotten the spare tire on."

"Lucky you," she said. "With my luck, I would have had a bunch of old grannies stop by to give me a hand, and we'd have been stuck there forever."

They both laughed at that.

"Oh, this guy was pretty nice," Sammy admitted. "Not sure what he is doing in the area, but I think he's in one of the rental places up there," she said, as she gave an arm motion off toward the corner.

"Maybe that was him in the trees outside," Annie said. "Maybe he really liked you."

"Well, that's not the way to a woman's heart," Sammy said quietly. "In fact, it's the absolute opposite." And she sure as hell hoped that wasn't Eton out there. That would give her nightmares now for the rest of the night. She looked at her friend and said, "Thanks for that."

Annie gave her a clipped nod. "Tit for tat," she said. "If I won't sleep, why should you?"

And the two of them both went off to bed, cuddling their hot chocolate, feeling a little jumpy. It would be what it would be, but at least they were together.

ETON RACED TO the vehicle and sped off to the other

village. He had his GPS up and running on his phone in the seat beside him, as he tried to get to where the cell phone activity was happening. If they could at least pinpoint it and see what people were there, it would help a lot. He knew that Ice had some satellite work going on here too, but that didn't mean it was up and running, that it was pointed in the right area, that heavy tree cover could interfere, or that they would find anything. But Eton would work on this end too.

He hit the other village and moved toward the location that Garret had given him. The road had several twists—a left turn, right turn, and then another right turn. Before he knew it, he was up against what looked like a set of townhomes. He swore softly, picked up the phone, and dialed Garret. "It's a multifamily townhome complex," he said. "Looks pretty high-end."

"Which doesn't mean anything," Garret said, his voice distracted. "I'm getting the reading from the building, but I can't lock it down any closer than that. Normally we can't even get that close. It's usually within a block or two."

"Well, in that case, that's as close as you'll get because it looks like trees are all around this complex," Eton said.

"Plus the person we are tracking could be out walking among the trees for that very reason," Garret said. "Remember that."

Eton replied, "Yeah, just because we're here at the townhome complex doesn't mean he lives here. I'll get out and walk around." He parked the vehicle in the guest parking lot and hopped out. "Most of the parking spaces here are empty. Maybe it's not quite filled up for sales yet?"

Garret replied, "I'm checking to see what the status is of the building. It might be newly completed."

"I'd say it is still in progress," Eton said. "Supplies are

still stacked off on the side, and a couple big trucks—one flatbed—and lots of pickup trucks are here, as if the work isn't quite completed."

"I wonder if anybody is living there," Garret muttered, as his fingers tapped away on the keys. "It's possible that it's someone who bought early," he said, "but now we've opened up possibilities of it being anybody, even a worker there."

"Or anyone who just knows this building is in progress and could easily be utilizing it too," he said.

"It's fairly close to the top of the hill, as far as reception goes."

"Good point," Eton said. "I'll go up to the top and take a look for myself."

"Are any trails there?" Garret asked.

"None that I see at this point." Eton dashed through trees and rough underbrush to find an easier way up. "I'm trying to stay in the trees, but there isn't an easy way through some of them without attracting attention."

"You could walk along the edge," Garret suggested.

"I could, but then I'm running the risk of somebody else out here seeing me."

"It's a catch-22, isn't it?"

"Maybe not," he said. "Looks like I see a trail, not well used, likely an animal trail."

"Well, go easy, if there is a trail, and if another guy is out there, he's likely to be on it too."

"Good," Eton said. "It would be nice if we could catch a break for once."

"No kidding, right?"

As Eton headed out on the trail, he listened for any sounds around him. "The night's really quiet," he said in a low voice.

"Meaning?"

"Nothing is stirring," he said. "I would expect animal life of some kind."

"It's a bit early though, isn't it?"

"Birds?"

"A bit late for that," Garret said. "I'm not too sure about the birds around here though."

"I think birds around here are much wiser than we are used to."

"It's hard to say, but you could be right," Garret replied. "Just keep an eye out."

"No problem there," he said. "Last thing I want is to have a sniper take me out before I get anywhere."

"Really didn't need to think about that one," Garret said, with a note of humor.

"Doesn't change the fact that, if somebody is here and knows that we are too, we're in trouble."

"I don't think anybody has our location here yet," he said.

"Are they running decoys in Australia?"

"Decoys all over the place at this point," he said.

"Good," Eton said. "Let's hope they don't get shot either."

"Right, that's not part of the plan," he said, "but you can never really tell what the hell is going on."

"I know." He crested the top of the hill and muttered into the phone, "I'm up at the top now."

"Good. Take a look around," Garret said. "I'm still getting the signal. Let me track your location and see how close I can get."

"You should get pretty close," he said, "and I'm on the top of the hill, so maybe that will help you identify where the signal is coming from at least."

"Maybe," he said, but his voice was distracted once again.

Eton searched through the darkness, looking for signs of anybody out there. He couldn't see anything, but that didn't mean much at this point. As he waited and watched, he tried to adjust to the silence around him. He absolutely adored silence, but it was weird to actually get it. There was nearly always buzzing from electrical appliances or lights, traffic noises, and, of course, people.

At the very least, he would have expected sounds of animal life up here. But, since he'd arrived, it was like all the birds had stopped and were now watching him instead. Hopefully they were also watching anybody on the other side. Eton was hoping to contact somebody, well, as in to capture somebody—whoever it was and whatever phone he had in use—in order to figure out who else was after him and his team.

So far it hadn't been terribly easy finding clues, and, every time they got to their prey, he was often already dead or was dead within minutes. That was a problem Eton had to deal with, too because it was frequently his own fault that he was coming up against bodies. He had a tendency to shoot first and to ask questions later. It worked a lot of times but not when you needed answers. And that was definitely a problem right now.

Eton moved from tree to tree, as silent as the night around him. But it didn't take long to realize that the wedge of a hill that he was on extended in both directions, probably for miles. But he was currently at the closest point to the condos down below. He stopped and studied them, looking for lights, looking for anything. He put his phone on Silent and sent a text to Garret. **No lights on at the condos.**

Not inhabited yet, Garret responded. **Fully sold, not yet able to move in.**

The vehicles?

Company trucks.

Dead end?

No, Garret typed. **The signal is still coming, but again the perimeter is wider than we would like.**

I'm not seeing anything up here. Maybe I'll go down and take a look inside the condos.

Do that, Garret typed. **But watch your back.**

Eton picked his way down the hill, once again keeping his movements silent and as simple as possible. By the time he reached a large jump off, where there was framework for a retaining wall but no roof yet, he managed to scramble on top and jump down to the concrete. He landed a little more heavily than he would have liked.

As he waited here, crouched in the darkness, no lights came on, and no sounds emerged, suggesting no one heard him. He quickly made his way toward the building, happy to see it wasn't at the total lock-up stage, so it was easy to get inside. There were definitely locks on doors, but one of the garages was open. He stepped inside and made his way through that condo. A quick search told him that they were at the finishing-up stage. Drywall was installed; paint was being applied. He made his way into four of the homes, but the other four were locked. He checked the windows and found them not secured. He quickly scanned the rest. By the time he was done, he stepped outside and texted Garret that nobody was here.

Garret quickly replied. **The signal stopped then started again from the same direction. Is anything else around you?**

A couple single-family houses, about a two-minute walk away.

So, on your way up, you passed a dirt road, Garret texted. **It leads to two houses.**

I'll check that out.

Eton made his way back to his vehicle and, without his headlights on, slowly drove down the road, until he saw the dirt road that Garret mentioned. As it was, a grove of trees was farther down. He pulled off the main road and parked in there, then got out and walked back to the dirt drive. He headed along that road but immediately heard dogs barking. He sent a message to Garret, telling him dogs were nearby.

So much for getting in silently.

Wasn't that the truth? Dogs were great for this kind of thing, if they were on your side. But it was pretty shitty now, when Eton didn't want anybody to know he was here. He got as close as he could without triggering any further alarms, but he was still outside the gates on one house, and another gate farther up showed more dogs at the second house. He quickly sent back a message. **Dogs at both.**

Might as well come home then. We'll do more research first.

With that, Eton turned and headed back to his car. As he reached his vehicle and was just about to get in, he heard the sounds of a vehicle driving toward him, coming down from the condos. He disappeared into the tree growth and waited. The other vehicle slowed down when it got to his, and it looked like somebody was checking the license plate. He quickly sent Garret a message about it and received an immediate reply.

Interesting. And you didn't see anybody at the condos, right?

Right.

They were watching you maybe?

Quite possibly.

Come on home.

That's the plan. Eton waited in the darkness for the single driver to pull away, but it seemed like he was more concerned about standing there and taking a photo. If Eton had been on guard duty at the townhomes, he'd have done the same thing because security never wanted something like this to happen without at least checking it out. What Eton didn't know was who this guy was and why he was doing it. He wondered about jumping forward and saying something but decided that wasn't a good idea. As soon as the driver got in his vehicle and drove away again, Eton sent a message back to Garret, saying he was doing a quick switch of vehicles.

Good enough.

Eton headed toward the town, looking for an option. When he got there, the place seemed to be just as dead as it had been before. If not more so. A couple lights were on in the small town, but that was it. As he passed the road heading toward his place, he remembered where Sammy had said she'd been, at her friend's house. He wondered if a small shopping center was up ahead, but it was mostly just three or four stores, and, with all the businesses closed right now, he saw no sign of any other vehicles. He would have to drive into the major city center. With that, he quickly made a U-turn and headed out.

He could make it back again in an hour, as long as he booked it. And now that his vehicle had been spotted, he didn't have any reason or excuse for being up here and had no cover. So getting another vehicle immediately was really the only option. As he drove, he sent a message to Garret.

We shouldn't stop searching yet.

We won't. We still are.

Maybe. But I'm on the way to switch out, so I'll be back in an hour or two.

With that, he rang off, still wondering what the hell that guy was doing and where he'd been. Had Eton been made, or was it just his vehicle that had been made? So many questions, and, of course, never any answers.

CHAPTER 5

S AMMY WOKE UP the next morning with an odd sense of disconnect. Then she remembered that Annie was here with her. She got up, walked into the bathroom, and had a quick hot shower. Coming out, she dried off, got dressed, put her hair in a braid, and headed downstairs to put on coffee. Annie was in the first-floor guest room and would likely sleep in late. But Sammy was an early riser. She was still a little out of sorts from seeing not only Eton and another man up on the hill but also seeing a stranger outside her house. No need for it. That was the one thing that bothered her.

Why would anybody care that she was here with her father? Unless she'd been followed, after picking up Annie. And that was a little disconcerting too. She didn't want to get in between Annie and her ex, but somebody had slashed Sammy's tire as well, so she'd already been targeted, or maybe she'd just been unlucky in her location, and this was really all about Annie. That would make more sense.

Sammy frowned, as she thought about it. Shit, no real way to compare the silhouette she'd seen to that of Annie's husband. Because they were both very tall and slim, and, true enough, her husband used to wear a lot of hoodies. But then if somebody were to place blame on Annie's husband, that was an easy answer, yet not necessarily the truth. But there must be a reason for that tire slashing and stalking too. And it would also mean that somebody was after either her or Annie. To think that there would be two potential threats was a bit of a stretch for her.

All in all, it gave her an odd feeling, but she went ahead and put on the coffee and set out breakfast for her father. In the mornings he usually liked to have slices of fresh bread, sometimes maybe an egg or two. She wandered toward his room and listened, and, when she didn't hear anything, she called out, "Papa, are you there?"

His rumbling voice answered her.

She smiled and said, "Coffee is on." Then she headed back to the kitchen, her heart pounding, as she realized that his days were numbered. Still, what she could do was remember to enjoy the moments that she had with him. As she headed downstairs to the kitchen, Sammy heard his door open, and he came in behind her.

"I had a good night," he said, with a bright smile. "What about you?"

She gave him a nod. "Yeah, except for Annie," she said. "She called, looking for a place to stay last night."

Immediately his face twisted in concern. "Problems?"

"Not sure," she said. "I would have told you about it yesterday, but I didn't want to disturb you."

He raised his eyebrows, then frowned.

"Just that, after I'd been over there visiting, I hadn't driven too far and got a flat tire. It was such a clean cut that I was wondering if somebody had done it on purpose. Then, when Annie and I spoke last night, I found out that her tires had been slashed too."

The look on his face hurt her.

She rushed over and said, "I'm fine, Dad. Honest. I was

just trying to figure out what to do from here," she said.

"Do you have the cut tire?"

"I do," she said. "I need to take it and get it fixed because, at the moment, I don't have a spare."

He nodded. "Maybe you should drive my vehicle," he said worriedly.

She reached out, patted his cheek, and said, "No need. If I have to, then I will, but, at the moment, mine is working just fine."

He nodded. "And Annie?"

"She spent the night," Sammy said. "She was pretty unnerved, and I just thought I would give her a good night's sleep."

"You're a good friend," he said, with a bright smile.

"Well, we'll see about that," she said, with a cheeky look. "I might put her to work."

He rolled his eyes. "You should go for lunch somewhere," he said. "Have some fun and do something besides working all the time. You don't do enough of that."

"I do just fine," she said, laughing.

He sat down on the table, looking at the bread. "I do love this bread," he said, as he cut himself a big thick slice and slathered fresh butter all over the top.

She watched him, a smile growing on her face. "Do you want eggs or just some jam?"

"Cheese," he said. "I'd love some cheese."

"Good enough," she said and brought over the cheese that they had in the fridge. She sat down with a cup of coffee, and he looked at her. "You won't eat?"

"I thought I'd wait for Annie," she explained.

Immediately he nodded. "That's a good idea." He grinned at her. "More for me that way!"

She laughed. "I wish you would get all that bread down," she said. "You've cut your appetite in half these days."

"Just not that hungry," he said.

She nodded. "I know, but it concerns me anyway."

"You would worry no matter what," he said, with a knowing smile.

She shrugged and agreed. "That's what happens when you love somebody," she said, chuckling.

"You should have a partner," he said abruptly.

She winced at that. "How about we just don't go in that direction?" she said, shaking her head.

"Maybe, but you know it's true," he replied.

"Well, the right guy hasn't walked across my path just yet," she said. "So what would you have me do?"

"I don't understand it," he said. "You're beautiful. You're smart. You're intelligent. So what's the problem?"

She laughed. "What makes you think there is a problem?" she asked.

"Always seems to be something," he said. "Are the guys blind out there?"

"Yes, maybe," she cheerfully said. This was an old argument between the two of them.

"I'm sorry that last guy didn't work out."

"I'm not," she said, "because, when you really think about it, he obviously wasn't someone I needed in my life."

"Maybe," he said, "but still it would be nice to have a partner. I could leave you happily."

"Meaning, there would be a man to take care of me," she teased. "Oh, please, you know me better than that."

He gave her that big grin of his.

"But it doesn't change the fact," she said, "that some

things I just can't change."

"No," he said, "that's not true. Maybe somebody would get smart enough to find gold where it is, instead of just looking at all the other pretty things that walk by. Shiny isn't a measure of substance."

"Maybe that is a lesson I need to learn," she said lightly, picking up her big mug and taking a sip.

He looked at her, his gaze sharpened. "Maybe," he admitted. "Relationships aren't easy at the best of times. They take work."

"And here I thought you and Mom had it made," she said. "No work there."

"We had our moments," he said, with a grin. Then he looked at the loaf of bread, shook his head, and said, "You know what? I think I'll have a little more."

She watched, as he cut himself a second big slab and covered it in honey this time. She got up and refilled his coffee cup, then heard sounds of movement. "Sounds like Annie is awake," she said.

"Great," he said. "I'd like to see her. Been a long time since she was here."

"Well, not so long," she said gently, "she was here last week."

He recovered quickly and said, "But she didn't stay long."

Annie came in just at that time. She looked at the two of them, smiled, and said, "Did I miss breakfast?"

"No, not at all," her father said, turning with a big smile. "My, aren't you looking lovely this morning."

She chuckled, walked over, gave him a kiss on the cheek, and said, "Ever the charmer."

"Of course," he said. "Some things just come naturally."

Annie chuckled and sat down at the table, until she spied the coffee. Then she bounced to her feet, walked to the cupboard, where she snagged herself a cup and filled it. Looking back, she asked, "Anybody else need some?"

"I just refilled ours," Sammy said. "Did you get any sleep?"

Annie gave her a look and shrugged.

"Right, same as me," she said.

"It's a little tough when you are unsettled," she said diplomatically.

"Very true."

Annie came over to the table again, sat down, and looked at the bread. "Now that looks lovely too. May I?"

Embarrassed at forgetting her manners, Sammy hopped up and proceeded to make breakfast for the two of them.

When it was done, they cleaned up, and her father headed upstairs to work. Annie asked, "Can I trouble you for a ride home?"

"Absolutely," she said. "Did you arrange for a tow for your car yet?"

"Not yet," she said. "I'll do it when I got home."

"And maybe we should talk to the cops," Sammy said quietly. "If it is your ex, he shouldn't be allowed to get away with this."

"You know what? I don't really want to bring more trouble onto my head," she murmured.

"I get it, but that doesn't mean that avoiding the issue will make it any better." Her friend wrinkled up her nose and nodded. "Maybe you'd feel better if I'm there when you talk to the police," Sammy said, and that's what they did. They waited an extra twenty minutes before leaving because the cops wouldn't be at Annie's right away.

Finally, by the time they were leaving, Annie looked at her and said, "Should I say goodbye to your dad?"

"Don't bother," she said. "He isn't likely to remember anyway."

"I'm so sorry," she said. "That's got to be hard."

"It's horrible," she said, "but it is what it is, and I'm trying to make peace with it."

"You are a better person than I am," Annie said. "I would rant and rave to the skies."

"That won't do me any good. Besides, so far the skies have yet to answer back."

At that, and still chuckling, the two walked out of the house. She drove her friend quickly home, and the police arrived as she pulled up.

Annie said, "You need to tell them about your car too."

Sammy hesitated, but Annie shook her head. "What's good for me is good for you," she warned.

Groaning, but with a grin, Sammy hopped out of the vehicle and walked over to the cops, as Annie quickly explained the little bit she knew. And then Sammy explained about her tire too. It wasn't in the trunk unfortunately to show them. But they could already see the destruction on Annie's car. They took what little information they had and then left. She looked at Annie. "You good to go?"

"Absolutely." Annie turned and walked back into the house.

Sammy hesitated for a long moment, wondering if she should follow her, but it didn't seem to make any sense. Then she turned, got back into her vehicle, and drove off. She had a long day of work ahead of her, and, without any sleep, it would be just that much harder to get through it.

As she headed up the main road to her driveway, she saw

another vehicle coming toward her. She immediately slowed down, wondering who it was. They didn't have very many strangers here as it was, but, with the odd events happening now, she couldn't help but look to see who it might be. Sure enough, it was Eton, but he was driving a completely different vehicle.

She gave him a good frown, but he gave her a city smile and waved as he drove on. She pulled onto the road that she needed, but her mind was consumed, wondering why he changed vehicles and what had happened to the other one?

IT TOOK ETON a moment to realize that his new vehicle was probably causing Sammy some concern. But he already had multiple excuses ready when needed. Right now he was heading into town, looking for information from various storekeepers. But he was also going on the pretense of shopping. He pulled in outside the butcher, walked in, looking for fresh bacon. And, sure enough, there was some. He bought a little bit and struck up a conversation. "Is there much business with all these little towns around here?" he asked.

The butcher nodded. "We have our regulars," he said. "Other than that, not likely. But I'm the only butcher around for the next couple towns, so I get other surrounding business too."

"That's good," he said. "I thought the other town or the one over from here was bigger than this one?"

"Not really," he said. "It's a little bit bigger, but they are all spread out," he said. "So population-wise, we are the same. Most businesses need the population from all these towns around here to stay in business," he said. "It's not like in the olden days."

"I guess a lot of people here are commuters, aren't they?"

"Yes." He looked at him and asked, "What are you doing here? Just a tourist?"

Eton nodded. "Yes," he said, "staying at one of the chalets for a few days. A bunch of buddies got together." He looked at the bacon and said, "Considering that, you want to double up the bacon for us?"

The butcher nodded.

"I think I saw something about condos for sale around here somewhere. Do you know anything about that?" he asked. "The guys and I are really enjoying being out in the country."

"Those condos have been a nightmare for the area," the butcher said, with a headshake. "It was a go five years ago, then they shut it down. It's been one of those on-again, off-again deals," he said, with a shake of his head.

"I don't understand these property developers," Eton said. "You'd think people would get their facts straight, before they got to that point."

"You'd think so," he said, "but then people will be people."

"Is it all being done by locals? That aspect would be a nice shot in the arm for the economy."

"No, of course not," he said, with disgust. "I think they hire one or two local guys for security up there overnight, but that's it."

"Yeah, probably guys who don't really have regular jobs maybe?"

"Not all. I think old Joe over there took on one of the jobs, looking for extra money for his grandkid."

"That's a nice thing to do," Eton said.

"That's the guy Joe is though," he said.

Eton nodded. "Is there a problem with the grandkid?"

"Yeah, he's got some leg issues that need surgery, and he needs equipment to help him recover, so Joe was picking up some shifts, trying to raise some of that money."

"Well, if it wouldn't insult him," Eton said, "I'll be happy to donate a little bit. I mean, I don't have a ton, but anything would help a family like that."

The butcher looked at him warily, but his gaze warmed considerably. "Well, he's right over there in the coffee shop. You can go talk to him about it, if you like."

He looked over to see an older man, sitting there outside. "That's him at the table?"

"It is," he said.

"I'll go do that." Paying for his bacon, he smiled and walked out to the street. As he crossed the road, he walked into the little coffee shop, ordered a coffee, and took it outside. He looked at the man seated there and asked, "Are you Joe?"

Joe stared at him and said, "Yeah."

"I was just talking with the butcher," he said. "He mentioned you were working up at that condo project, doing some night security work to raise money for your grandkid."

"Yeah, he ought to stick to butchering."

Eton motioned at the chair and asked, "Do you mind if I sit down for a moment?" Joe looked at him, then the chair and just shrugged. "I'm sorry that your grandkid is having some issues."

"It's my grandson," he said. "And the butcher talks too much."

"My fault probably because I was asking questions," he said. "So I'm interested in helping out a little. I don't have a ton of money, but, if a few dollars would help out, to make things a little easier," he said, "I'm up for it."

Joe looked at him in surprise. "Why would you do that?"

"Because not everybody in the world is an asshole," Eton said sincerely.

At that, Joe burst out laughing. "You could have fooled me," he said. "The bastards could have covered the thing with the medical insurance, but they wouldn't. The surgery itself is covered but not the equipment he needs at the other end. And you can't do one without the other, so it's off until we can raise the money."

"Must be tough having to go back to work after you've retired."

"It is, and it sucks too. It's not just tough. My bones like to stay abed at nighttime, not chasing strangers driving up all those roads."

"Strangers?"

"Yeah, there's been traffic up and down that damn place. You'd think they'd let us security guards get a decent nap, but, no, of course not."

"Strangers? Can't be too many of those around here."

"Well, you are one of them, now that I think about it," he said.

Eton immediately introduced himself and explained where they were staying.

"Ah, yeah, we often get people from that Airbnb stuff," he said. "It's all garbage."

"Well, it looks like a good source of income for people who need it," he said.

"Maybe, maybe the people don't just need it, they want it," he said. "I've come to understand that *needs* and *wants* are very different things at this point in my life."

"I'm sorry. That's a hard lesson to learn, isn't it?"

"Well, I learned it," he said. "I just didn't expect to have to do it again."

Eton pulled some cash from his wallet and handed over four hundred dollars and said, "Put this toward the expenses," he said. "Let's get that boy on the road to recovery." With that, he picked up his coffee, smiled at Joe, and said, "I hope you have a better day."

Joe nodded, as he accepted the money, clearly flustered. "Thank you. I don't know what to say. Thank you."

"Not an issue," Eton said, as he took his leave. He decided that maybe, instead of continuing to ask around, he'd drive a little farther into another town and start looking for answers there. One thing was for sure; he needed a new source now. He didn't want to cause any alarms locally. He wasn't ready to stop checking things out though.

As he walked back to his car, Joe called out to him. Eton turned back and looked at him. He couldn't hear the old man, so he walked back, saying, "I'm sorry. I couldn't hear you. What did you say?"

"I was just saying thank you again," he said. "Getting a little closer every day, and maybe, pretty soon, I'll leave that bloody security job."

"The condos are almost done anyway, aren't they?" he asked. "Surely they don't need the security guards for much longer?"

"Maybe not," he said. "I don't much like being up there. People are walking around in the dark, where they shouldn't be."

"Did you tell the bosses that?"

"I did, but they won't do anything about it," he said.

"Well, if you think there is any danger, it's sure not

worth risking your life for," Eton said in all seriousness. "Surely they are at the lock-up stage by now. And then, if someone breaks in up there, it's an insurance matter."

The security guard looked at him for a long moment and nodded. "Maybe I'll have a talk with them."

"Are you there all night?" Eton asked.

Joe shook his head. "Midnight to six."

Eton managed a completely honest grimace on his face. "Not my ideal time to work," he said. "Especially outside."

"That's exactly the problem," he said. "My old body isn't meant to do that anymore."

"Well, I mean, if you need the money, then it's certainly understood," he said, "but, if you can make your way without doing those hours, it will be better for you."

"Isn't that the truth? Still, I'll have to think about it."

"But, if you think you're in any danger, you can call the police, right?"

He shrugged and said, "Well, I won't." He shook his head. "It would take hours for them to get there, especially at that time of night."

At that, Eton stopped, then walked over, and, pulling a little notepad out of his pocket, he jotted down his cell phone number. "You can always call me, while we're here anyway," he said. "I've got special ops and militarily background," he said, "and I could get there pretty quickly. Don't put your life in danger."

There must have been enough sincerity in his voice for the other man to believe him because he took the note and nodded. "I sure don't want to quit, if I don't have to," he said.

"Good enough," he said. "Just give me a call, if you run into any trouble up there. I don't mind at all."

"Maybe you're the trouble," Joe said, only half joking.

"And because you don't know me, I understand that," he said, "but a lot of people will vouch for me."

"What are you doing around here?"

"Hunting," he said, with half a smile and a glance over his shoulder. "Looking for some of those guys you don't ever want to meet in the dark."

At that, Joe looked at him, his gaze sharp.

Eton, breaking his long-standing rule of not talking about his job, nodded. "I'm serious," he said. "If you think even for a minute that anything is going on up there, just let me know, and I'll come running."

"I don't want to get killed over this."

"Exactly," Eton said in a quiet voice. "Remember your priorities too. That boy needs his grandpa. It's not worth getting killed over."

"Damn it. I figured it was nothing," he said, staring off in the distance, "but then, last night, a couple of them were around."

"A couple what?"

"A couple guys," he said, "and that made me aware that something else was happening up there."

"Do you think it's the staff from the jobsite?"

"No," he said, "I don't think it's like that at all. He's always talking to somebody."

"Weird," Eton said, staring out, but it certainly lined up. "Like I said, don't put yourself in a position where you could be in danger."

"I think that's what they expect of me though."

"Are they paying you enough for that?"

The old man shook his head.

"You have already reported the problem to management,

right?"

Joe nodded.

"Tell them that, as long as all this shit is going on up there, with strangers walking around in the dark, you want nothing to do with it."

"I'll see," he said.

It was obvious the old man was thinking about his grandson and what needed to happen with him. Eton had done what he could at least. "Call me. Anytime at all," he said, and, with that, he walked away. He could only do so much, before it didn't make a bit of a difference anymore, and people were better off making their own decisions. He hoped he'd made the right one in telling Joe. And he especially hoped Joe made the right decision and called him if anything went south. Very little room for recovery when people went down the wrong pathway. Sometimes you get no room to recover, and things go straight downhill very quickly. That's not what Eton wanted for Joe.

CHAPTER 6

B Y THE END of the day, Sammy was tired and worn out. They'd had nothing but problems at work. Several designs needed to be dealt with, and her dad was having a difficult day. He'd gone to have a nap at two, and, by four, he still hadn't gotten up. Worried, she'd gone into his room to find him completely disoriented, sitting on the side of the bed. She tapped him, and he got up and followed her into the kitchen to have a cup of coffee. When he finally got his thoughts back together again, he looked up at her with sad eyes and said, "It's getting worse, isn't it?"

She'd frozen, then reached over, gave him a hug, and said, "It doesn't matter, Dad. You have enough to worry about. Don't worry about that too."

He reached up, patted her hand, and said, "I think that's my line."

Now the two of them had returned to the office upstairs. He sat beside her, staring at the diagrams, not necessarily helping but not hurting either. And she enjoyed having him here. "You do good work," he muttered, as he watched her.

"I learned from the best," she said, with a smile.

He chuckled. "I don't know about that," he said. "This getting old sucks."

She didn't say anything because there wasn't anything she could say. It might suck, but she suspected it didn't suck this much for everybody. But then maybe that was just her naive idea about aging. "We'll get through it together," she promised.

He reached over again to pat her hand, then picked up a pencil and went to work. She watched him carefully for a few minutes, without letting him see, then realized that he really was there and was doing a great job; so she settled back to continue on her own work. By the end of the day, he said, "I'm not even hungry."

"Well, you shouldn't be too tired," she said. "You had a good nap this afternoon."

"But I am," he said. "Maybe I'll just go lie down."

She watched in worry as he got up and headed to his bedroom again.

"What about you?" he asked, stopping at the doorway. "Will you stop and eat?"

She hadn't been planning on it, but, as he'd asked a direct question, she shrugged and said, "Maybe."

"No maybe about it," he said. "You need food."

"Well, if you don't, I don't," she said in exasperation.

He just glared at her.

She shrugged. "It takes two."

"If I eat, will you eat?"

"Deal," she said and hid a smile. He just glared at her. She looked at him gently and added, "We have to do what we have to do."

"Fine," he said. And he walked back over to where she sat. "Can we eat sooner?" he asked hopefully.

"We can," she said. "Any particular wishes?" When he named one of her pasta specialties that he'd loved forever, she smiled. "It'll take a little bit of time to make though," she said.

Immediately he changed his mind, and she shook her head. "I don't mind the work," she said, "but you have to stay awake."

"I will," he said. "I'll even come help."

So together they put away their architectural drawings and went down to the kitchen. As she started working on what was essentially homemade pasta, but a much easier version just dropped into boiling water in little pieces, she wondered that she hadn't heard from Annie.

Almost as if he were listening to her thoughts, her father asked, "What about Annie?"

"Good question," she said. "I was just thinking about her. But there doesn't appear to be any calls from her." She checked her cell phone again and shrugged.

"Good. No news is good news," he said.

"I hope so," she said. "It does make me a little worried though."

"I'm sure she's fine," he said casually. He was getting the boiling water ready, putting the salt in it. "How is that dough coming along?"

"It's doing great," she said, giving the spongy batter a hard stir.

He looked over and smiled. "You always were a good hand with that dish."

"Because we love it so much, I have lots of practice making this one," she said brightly. She leaned over, gave him a kiss on the cheek. "Anything for the special man in my life." Immediately she realized she shouldn't have brought that up because he frowned at her, and the scolding began.

"You need to have a partner, a man who would be there for you."

"Well, if and when I find one," she said, chuckling, "I'll

be sure to let you know."

"It's not that funny," he said. "Being alone sucks."

"I know," she said. "You fill the gap though, so there's been no void in my life for a very long time."

"That's not good either," he said, with a shake of his head.

She chuckled and said, "Are you chopping and frying that bacon, so we'll have layers here or what?"

With that, he completely devoted himself to the next project, and, after they had the dish in the oven, completely slathered with sweet cheese, he looked at her and said, "That smells so good."

"Twenty minutes," she said. "That's all we need, twenty minutes."

He nodded. "I'll set the table."

He worked on that, as she cleaned up the dishes from preparing the dish. It's not that it had to be a big mess, but somehow she always ended up with one. She didn't understand that. Her mother could cook up a storm, and the kitchen always looked great. In Sammy's case, the dish looked great too, but, by the time she was done cooking, a huge mess awaited her in the kitchen. She cleaned up, and, by the time she was done, the table was set, and now the cheese had melted, and the casserole was thoroughly heated. Her father opened a bottle of wine, and she brought out dinner. He was seated at the table, and, just as she was about to join him, her phone rang. She looked at it and frowned.

"You going to answer that?" her father asked, as he picked up the great big serving spoon and served himself a hefty scoop.

She smiled at the amount. That was a lot of food for somebody who supposedly wasn't hungry. "I will," she said.

"I just don't know the number."

He peered over and said, "Oh, *Private Caller*, huh? A secret admirer?"

"I doubt it," she said, and, when she went to answer it, nobody was there. She shrugged and said, "Must have been a wrong number."

"Oh, he'll call back," her father said, with a wink. She smiled, and, when the phone did ring again, she planned to ignore it, until she saw Annie's name. She answered it and put it on Speakerphone. "Hello, Annie. I'm here with Dad, having dinner. How are you?"

"I'm okay," she said, but her voice was shaky.

"Something else happen?"

"Well, I was followed home from town today," she said. "At least I think so. I'm starting to feel paranoid."

"Well, sometimes it's for a good reason," she said. "We don't want you to make light of something that's important."

"That's not helping me much," she said.

"No, it probably isn't, and I'm sorry. I'm not sure what to say," she said. "What kind of a vehicle was it?"

"It was a truck, like my ex's."

"But did you recognize him?"

"No," she said. "I didn't. That's the thing. It was just a big truck. Anybody could have had been driving it."

"Well, lots of people do have them," she said. "We can't go looking for boogeymen where there aren't any."

"But what if there are, and I didn't see it coming?" she cried out.

"Are you home now?"

"Yes, my vehicle was taken by the garage, and new tires put on. They sent a courtesy car to pick me up when it was ready."

"That was nice," she said. "And now you are home again with good tires, right?"

"Yes, all good, except for the cost," she said. "That was not cheap. It pisses me off. I don't have that kind of money."

"Not many people do," she said, "so there's lots of things to consider."

"I know. Anyway I just thought I'd let you know I was home." With that, her friend hung up.

Frowning, she looked at her father and shrugged. "You heard as much as I did, but I don't know what to make of it."

"Sounds like that husband of hers is getting to be a headache."

"Possibly," she said, "but we don't know that for sure."

"The trouble with this scenario," her father said, "is you won't know anything until it's too damn late."

She winced at that and said, "Well, let's hope not."

When her phone rang again, she looked at it and said, "It's a Private Caller again."

"Well, answer it," he urged.

She glared at him. "The first call was nobody."

"Doesn't mean this one is," he said. "You have to break out of your shell sometimes."

"I've broken out of my shell," she protested. He just rolled his eyes at her. She glared at him but answered the phone anyway. "Hello?"

"Sammy?"

The man's voice made her sit up straight. "Yes. Is this Eton?"

"It is," he said. "I just wanted to invite you out for coffee."

She stared at her father, who by now almost danced in place. "How did you get my number?" she asked.

"It's pretty easy to get from a directory. Remember the business I'm in?"

"I don't think I want to," she said. "It's a little creepy."

"Well, I figured it would be a long cold day before you'd give your number to me," he said, chuckling. "Remember? I'm harmless."

"Said the spider to the fly," she finished quickly.

At that, her father gasped in outrage and shook his head at her.

"Coffee could be nice," she said cautiously, "but why do I feel like there's an ulterior motive involved?" Again her father stared at her in shock. He reached over and spanked her lightly on her arm. "Fine," she said.

"Coffee at a little café in town, how is that?"

"When?" she asked, staring down at her dinner.

"Half an hour? How does that work for you?"

She thought about it, but her father was busy nodding his head. He leaned forward into the phone and said, "Perfect. She'll be there."

She gasped and quickly hung up the phone. "Seriously, Dad? Did you just do that?"

"You know I did," he said. "That poor guy could wait in the rain until he died from a chill before you'd have answered."

"I was getting around to it," she said defensively. "I try to think before I speak, you know?"

"Well, now you don't have to," he replied. She just rolled her eyes him. He motioned at her dinner. "You better eat up because you're just going for coffee. You might get a dessert down there, if they've been baking and didn't sell out." He frowned at her, thinking about that. "I haven't had anything from there in a long time."

"I can bring you back something, if you want," she said, with a gentle smile, because her father did love his sweets. "But remember. There is also still cake."

"Tea and cake," he said, his gaze immediately scanning the kitchen, as if looking for the cake.

"Dad, you're not getting cake until after dinner."

"Right," he said, looking down at his dinner. He picked up his fork and started shoveling it in, at a rate that was impossible to keep up. "You don't have to rush," she protested.

"Yes, I do, because you're leaving soon," he said, "and I don't like to eat without company."

Sometimes, nothing he said made any sense, but she just sat down and started eating her own plateful. By the time she was done, she looked at her dad and said, "I need to leave soon. I'll put on the teakettle and cut you a piece of cake before I go, okay?"

"Of course," he said, sitting back with a happy sigh. "That was excellent, as usual."

"It is a taste that is hard to let go of, once you get it in your mouth, isn't it?"

"Absolutely," he said.

She got up, put on the teakettle for him, rinsed out the teapot, and set it up with the tea bags, then walked over and put out the cake. She cut about a half-inch slice, and he said, "Now, if you'll make them small, you might as well cut me two."

She looked at him and said, "Or maybe I'm bringing you something."

He frowned at her and said, "I can have both."

Such a childlike quality was to his voice that she had to laugh. "You sure can," she said. "Besides, you did eat your dinner."

"I did," he said, with a happy smile.

She brought over a single piece of cake and said, "There is more over there, if you want it. I'll put it away when I get home tonight."

He nodded and said, "Be nice to him."

"Be nice to who?"

"The new boyfriend," he said, with a nod of satisfaction.

"I'm going for coffee, Dad," she said. "That's it."

"That's how they all start," he said. "Not to worry. If you're good and be quiet," he said, "you'll probably get there."

"Dad, if I have to be quiet, I'm not interested," she snapped. But he turned that big grin her way, and she realized that, once again, he'd been joking. Because of his illness, sometimes she didn't know when he was and when he wasn't, and, on a touchy topic like this, it was easy to take offense. She smiled. "You are trouble, mister."

"You love me anyway," he said comfortably.

"That I do." She raced back, gave him a big hug and a kiss, and said, "I won't be long."

"You can be as long as you like," he said. "I can't believe you're dating." And he started to raise his hands in a mock cheer. At that, she turned and raced from the house. This was the last thing she wanted to put up with. Her father meant well. She just wasn't into relationships if there wasn't a spark. And she also wasn't into relationships if there was *only* a spark. There had to be a whole lot more for her to want to go down that pathway. Especially now.

★

ETON DIDN'T KNOW why he'd had the compulsion to call her and to ask her out for coffee. Even Garret looked at him in surprise. Eton shrugged. "Just felt like it. I don't know why," he muttered by way of excuse.

"Well, maybe you can pump her for some information," Garret said, but there was a hesitation at *pump her*, a hesitation that had Eton glaring at him. Hands up in surrender, Garret said, "Honestly, she might know Joe. For real now."

Eton considered that and said, "I'll see how she is about talking, but I won't *pump her* for information," he said, with an exaggerated tone.

"Good," he said, "because that probably wouldn't get you anywhere. She seems like a nice quiet girl."

"She is," he said.

"Funny how just stopping like that to help her with a flat tire could do so much for you."

"No," he said, "it's not funny at all."

Garret grinned and said, "If it's a good bakery, I wouldn't mind a couple doughnuts or rolls and maybe a cinnamon bun too. Ever since I woke up out of that coma, I just want sugar."

"Which is the last thing you need," he said. "You should be home healing instead."

"News alert," Garret said. "I'm sitting here healing. It's hardly a hardship to do anything that I've been doing here right now."

"That's what bothers me," he said. "We're not getting anywhere, and I hate it. I just need to get outside these four walls for a bit."

"I was thinking about going up the mountain and seeing if we can change the frequency and maybe get a stronger signal."

"Maybe," he said. "We should also set up a similar one down here, in case he's on the move."

"I've already got most of that set up," he said. "You go off and have fun, while I work," he said and then laughed. "Listen to us. We sound like brothers."

"We are," Eton said seriously. "You know something? I wanted to howl when I heard what happened to you. We were so scared we would lose you," he said, his voice choking up with emotion.

Garret looked up at him and glared. "Don't you get emotional on me now," he said. "I don't like to cry."

"None of us like to cry, and we won't," he said. "No way in hell we will lose anybody from our team. Especially not when we don't know what happened to Bullard."

"The worst part is the not knowing," said Garret.

"I know," Eton said. "It really, really sucks."

"Exactly. But we have to stay strong, and we have to stay positive."

"Oh, I've got the positive part down," Eton said. "I'm damn sure I'll find some asshole, crack his head open over this mess, and, if you're feeling anything other than that, you should probably go home."

"You're not chasing me home," he said, "and I do feel like that, so don't you worry. Go have your little visit with the local girl," he said.

"It's hardly that," he said.

"Well, when you come back, you can tell me all about what it is then," he said, "because, from here, it sounds like something is there to me."

On that note, Eton turned and headed out. He couldn't explain the compulsion to get out, but he knew well enough he needed to honor it. Some things were just that way. It was a nice evening. The heat of the day had disappeared and had somehow given way to a cool breeze, a freshness to the air that he hadn't experienced earlier. The frustration was just eating at him. They hadn't run down any good leads or found anything they could tie to the case yet.

He was planning on going out to the townhome site tonight, just in case something was going on which Joe was caught up in the middle of, but it was also the place Eton and Garret were looking at themselves, so maybe somebody related to the attack on their team was going out there to make calls. Eton wanted to know about it, if they were, because he sure as hell wanted to find out who was behind this.

At the same time, they had just so many unknowns and so many factors they couldn't do anything about, and that it was driving him crazy. Getting out was just an excuse, but it also gave him a reason to call her. It hadn't been hard to find her. She'd been in the phone book under the architect's name, and that's what he planned on telling her. He pulled into town and parked on the street, loving how the lights lit up on the side. He wasn't even sure if the coffee shop was open at this hour. As he walked toward it, he was happy to see her sitting there outside, in the same place Joe had been.

"You know what?" he said. "I didn't consider whether this would even still be open in a small town like this."

"They do stay open, and he is the only one around who does," she said, with a smile.

He pointed at her coffee. "You wouldn't even let me buy that for you."

"I'm perfectly capable of buying my own drink," she said, chuckling. Just then a woman in an apron came out, carrying another cup and a large plate with a few treats. She put it down on the table, smiled at Sammy, and said to him, "This gal is a live one."

Sammy motioned and said, "This time, you see? I managed to buy you a drink."

"That's not fair," he said.

"It's the least I could do," she said, "after you helped me with the tire."

"I wish I could have helped you more," he said, sitting down, tickled that she'd thought about buying him a drink and snacks. "But you already had it well in hand before I got there."

"Well, maybe not," she said. "Apparently I'm not the only one who got her tire slashed."

His gaze sharpened, as he said, "Tell me more," and pulled the coffee closer to him. "And thank you for this," he added, lifting the cup. She smiled and nodded, then told him about Annie, her friend. "I guess people are people all around the world, aren't they?" he said sadly.

"I'm not exactly sure what you mean by that, but yes," she said.

He nodded. "So what is she doing about it?"

"She contacted the police today," she said. "When I drove her home, they were already there."

"Well, that's good," he said.

She nodded. "I just don't know what the deal is. Like if it's the ex-husband or not," she said.

"Was there that kind of violence in their world?"

"No," she said, "that's what surprises me. It was so out of character for him."

"So, if it's out of character for him, is there anybody else in her world that it would fit?"

She studied him for a moment and said, "I don't think so."

"Violence is like that," he said. "It's often not somebody we think could do it, unless we have a history of violence with them," he said. "And I don't mean to be cryptic. I'm just saying that sometimes we like to forget about the people around us who might have scared us at one time, but we didn't see enough violence to be worried about it."

She stared at him, shrugged, and said, "As much as I know her, I'm not sure who she has been seeing these days, as far as boyfriends, or even what she does during her days."

"So maybe that's one of the things you need to find out," he said, "because really? That can be everything."

"You're thinking that any new boyfriend could have set off the husband?"

"Yes," he said. "Does she have any other family?"

"She has family," she said, "but not close by. The nearest relative is several hours' drive away, I think."

"And whose house is it?"

"It's a rental, but it's the one she shared with her ex," she said slowly.

"Maybe the ex is still hoping to get back together with her, and seeing her with a boyfriend might have set him off. It could make him realize that he's losing her. Something like that is an easy way to pop a hair-trigger and to push him over the edge," he said.

"It's possible," she said. Sammy pulled out her phone and sent a text.

He watched as she did it. "Are you contacting her?"

"I am." She texted, just wondering if there could be anybody else in Annie's orbit. The response came back and was instant. Sammy picked up the phone and read off the response.

No, not dating anyone since last jerk stiffed me for lunch.

"Ask her how long ago?"

She did, and the answer came back right away.

Last week.

Sammy replied with another question. **Any chance somebody saw you there?**

No, I don't think so, why? Well, Jorge did.

"Shit," she said, as she looked at Eton. "Jorge saw her."

"And Jorge is?"

"The soon-to-be-ex," she said.

"Well, think about that then. What if he is still in love with her, still wants her in his life, then sees her with another man?"

"So it could have been him, is what you are thinking?"

"Oh, it certainly could have been," he said. "You have to consider it at least."

"Yes." She sent a message back. **What if he wanted to get back together with you and saw you with another man instead?**

That might do it, Annie responded.

Then Sammy's phone rang. She looked at him and apologetically said, "Sorry, but it's Annie calling."

He nodded and said, "Go for it." He looked at the plate and asked, "May I?"

She grinned and said, "Absolutely."

He looked at the treats and fancied a rounded pastry with nuts of some kind. He picked up one and took a bite and almost moaned. It was so good. As he studied the treats in front of him, something else caught his gaze, and he looked up to see her staring at him with heat in her eyes. Instantly he felt his own body reacting, and now, with his own gaze lit up another half-dozen degrees, her eyes widened. He'd caught her looking at him and realized just what that message had meant. She shook her head and pulled back. He smiled and didn't say anything, while she talked to Annie. Finally she hung up the phone.

"Annie is wondering if that's what it is," she said, "but we don't know for sure."

"Of course not," he said. "None of us could know, unless the police are staking out her place or following her around."

"True enough," she said. "But still, at the same time, it's odd, isn't it? Though she reminded me that he also just got the divorce papers."

"That would do it too. These things are often that way though," he said, "for a time. Then eventually everybody settles down."

She nodded, reached across, and picked up a treat from the plate. "So why are you really here?"

"I'm hunting," he said honestly. "Hunting people, a couple in particular, responsible for murders around the globe."

She gasped and stared at him in shock.

He said, "I'm not usually so honest about it, so please don't pass it around."

"I wouldn't," she said. "I'm not sure anybody would believe me anyway."

"Really? Well, that's not usually the response I get," he said, with a smile.

"What kind of response do you normally get?" she asked hesitantly.

"Shock, disbelief, laughter, any of the above."

"Well, that's not my response at all," she said. "I absolutely believe you. Just something about you makes it believable. So what were you doing up on the hill that night?"

"Reconnaissance," he said. "We were trying to triangulate a phone call that we knew was coming from two towns over. And that hill gave us the best reception."

She just studied him, but her jaw was closed.

He saw that she was weighing his words. She was an interesting enigma. Not like anybody he was accustomed to.

She nodded. "Interesting."

"Do you know anything about that condo group up around the corner here?"

"The one that Joe is looking after at night?"

He nodded.

"Only that it's had troubles off and on. Like they were building it, then they weren't, then they were again. Apparently now it's almost done," she said. "Why?"

"Joe said a bunch of funny stuff has been happening up there, and he doesn't feel terribly secure about it. I tried to get him to quit today, but he is thinking about his grandson."

She frowned at him. "How did you find out about Joe?"

"The butcher, then I went over and talked to Joe myself."

She slowly put down her coffee cup and the treat and said, "Seriously?"

"Why not?" he said. "I'm allowed to be human too."

"That's not what I meant," she said. "It's just that you're getting a lot of information on locals."

"I also like people," he said gently. "Again I'm no threat to you."

"So who are you a threat to?"

"The man who tried to kill several of my friends and potentially may have succeeded in killing one of them," he said. "He's still missing after his plane was blown up over the ocean."

"Ouch," she said. "It's not a very nice world at times."

"No, it's not," he said, "but it's the world around you. It's just that most people have the good fortune to be oblivious to it."

"But not you."

"No," he said, "not me. Most of my life it's been a case of *never me.*"

"Would you have liked a different line of work?"

He thought about that for a moment and said, "There are still assholes all around the world," he said. "I wouldn't particularly want to be responsible for capturing them," he said, "but neither do I want to leave anybody on their own against them." Just then his phone rang. With an eyebrow up, he pulled out his phone, looking at the screen. "Now isn't that interesting?"

"What?"

"It's Joe," he said. He held up one finger and answered. "Hello, Joe. What's up?"

"Well," he said, "I thought about what you were saying, and I can't afford to quit," he said hesitantly.

"I got that. And?"

"The thing is, I think that somebody has been hanging outside my house for the last few hours."

"Really? You think it's connected to your work?"

"They are hidden in the trees," he said, "so, if it's not connected to my work, I don't know what the hell it's connected to. I can't say I've lived a blameless life, but I sure haven't done anything to deserve this."

"Good enough," he said. "Give me your address, and I'll be there in a few minutes."

"No, I'm not sure you need to do that," he protested.

"Joe, there is a reason you called me," he said. "Just let me do what I need to do."

"If you're sure," Joe said doubtfully.

"I'm sure," he said.

Just then, Sammy reached a hand across, grabbed his wrist. "I know where Joe lives," she said, "I'll show you the way."

He looked at her and frowned, but her gaze was indomitable. "Okay, Joe. Sammy is here with me. We'll be there in a few minutes."

He heard the relief in the man's voice, as he said, "Okay, I'll expect you then."

Just as Joe started to hang up, Eton said, "Joe?"

Joe answered, "Yes?"

"Stay away from the windows," and then he hung up. He looked at her and said, "I'm sorry. I didn't plan on this being a date-slash-meeting, complete with field trip."

"Joe is a good guy," she said. "I don't want anything to happen to him."

He nodded and said, "Let's go." He tossed back the last of his coffee, stood, and motioned at hers. "Are you bringing that?"

She popped the last bite in her mouth and washed it down with her coffee. "Come on," she said. "Joe is only a few minutes away. I'll take you there."

"Why don't you just tell me how to get there?" he said. "I don't want to put you in any danger."

"No," she said, "that won't happen. I don't want you to scare Joe, and he is clearly already terrified, or he wouldn't have called you. So we'll go together."

He glared at her.

But she stood toe-to-toe with him and glared back. "Look. I'm not a wuss," she said, "and these are my friends and family you're talking about here. We are all family in this village. So, if some assholes are involved in murdering people, I want to make sure that you take them out of here, but we need to protect everybody here in the meantime."

"I get that," he said.

But she reached up, placed a finger against his lips. "Apparently you don't because you're still talking."

He threw up his hands. "You'll have to follow my orders."

"Right," she said sarcastically. "I'm not sure I've ever done that in my life."

As they walked toward his car, he said, "Are you always this difficult?"

"Absolutely," she said, laughing. "This is nothing."

He just shook his head.

"Bet you didn't know what you were getting into," she said, still laughing.

"Apparently, but it's all good," he said, with a smile.

She looked at his car and asked, "By the way, why are you in a different vehicle?"

"Do you want the very believable story I can tell you, or would you prefer the truth?"

"Always the truth," she said.

"Because the other one might have been seen by the wrong person."

She stopped, stared at him, then opened her mouth and closed it again. "Okay, I asked for the truth," she said, "so I guess I deserve that for an answer."

"And that's the truth," he said, with a smile.

CHAPTER 7

H EADING TO THE passenger side of Eton's car, Sammy wondered at his answer. The thing was, if he spoke the truth, then it was a reasonable answer. A part of her hoped he was joshing with her, but, from the set look on his face, she doubted it. She quickly gave him directions to where Joe lived.

"He's not far out of town, is he?" Eton murmured.

"None of us are," she said. "It's another reason we love living here. We are a very close-knit community. Except for this guy apparently." She thought this over for a while. "You said a couple towns over, right?" Frowning, she continued. "We pretty well know everybody within a certain vicinity, so it will be distressing if it's anybody I know."

"It's hard to say," he said. "We've got question marks for certain people, but we're not exactly sure who and what their involvement is, if any."

"Who?"

He hesitated.

"I've lived here all my life, Eton," she said. "If I can help you sort out the characters in this scenario, I'd be happy to."

He quickly mentioned the playboy with the sports car.

She snorted at that. "*Ugh.* He's an idiot," she said. "He might take money to do a job, but it would have to be a simple position because he really can't do anything more complicated."

"Okay," he said. "How simple?"

"Very. He could do the most basic of tasks. His focus is really on what's between his legs," she said dismissively.

"But, if he got into trouble, would he do something bigger in order to get out of it?"

She tilted her head and said, "He would do something bigger, if it meant elevating his lifestyle. He is really chafing at the bit because his parents cut back on his allowance."

"And he's got big car payments," Eton said.

She looked at him. "Is that thing not paid for?"

He shook his head.

"Well, in that case, he might do something stupid," she said. "Who else?"

"The owner of the security company."

"Yeah, well, that's another guy who is overly focused on his genitals."

"Did either of these guys come on to you?"

"Both," she said, with a wave of her hand. "Not my type."

"And just what is your type?" he asked.

"Not babies and not men who don't know how to handle themselves," she said.

He nodded. "Sounds good to me."

"Meaning?"

"I don't think anybody would put me in those categories," he said.

She smiled and said, "I agree. You are the last one I would think of along those lines."

"Thanks," he said, "that's a compliment."

"Well, if those two are the competition, the bar isn't all that high. Just sayin'."

He cracked up laughing, loving the spunk in this girl.

As he rounded a corner, she said, "That driveway up there leads to Joe's place."

Eton immediately shut off the lights and drove past the driveway. After they were well past, he turned around near the top of an incline, slowly drifting the vehicle downward.

"What are you doing?" she asked.

"I'll park, then get out and walk," he said. "Text Joe, and tell him we are outside, taking a look around."

She did, and, as soon as that was done, he pulled off onto the shoulder and said, "This is about as good of a hiding place as we'll get," he said.

"Yeah, and it's not much of one," she said.

"No, it sure isn't, but that's all there is."

"Okay," she said. "Now what?"

"Now we'll get out and walk," he said, "and this is when you have to pay attention to me and stay at my side. Otherwise, I'm leaving you here in the vehicle, and you'll have to lie down and hide."

She just stared at him.

"Right, so I guess you're staying with me," he said. "We'll quietly walk up the road and come across the property up at the highest elevation and then down to Joe's place. Did Joe answer you?"

She pulled out her phone and nodded. "Yeah, he sent me a thumbs-up."

"Good," he said. "Let's go take a look."

Just then her phone buzzed again. "Joe says the guy is up the hill."

"Perfect," he said. "Let's see if we can flush him out."

She hesitated, then he looked at her and said, "Your choices are to go into Joe's house, stay in the car, or come with me."

She frowned.

"Otherwise I'll make the choice for you."

"What would you prefer?"

"I would prefer you go into Joe's," he said.

"That's not a bad idea. He is pretty unnerved, isn't he?"

"He is, indeed, and with good reason."

"Okay." She hopped out and walked up the driveway, while Eton watched. He'd gotten out the same side of the vehicle, so he only had to open and to close one door, in case anybody was listening. Once outside, he smiled, as she walked up to Joe's door and knocked. Joe let her in, and, after she was safely inside, Eton raced up the road and around the corner.

Inside, Joe looked at her and asked, "Where is Eton?"

"He's checking out the hill up above."

Joe nodded with relief. "Good," he said. "I don't like a whole lot about this."

"Tell me what's going on," she said, and he filled her in on the strangeness going on during his overnight shift up at the townhome site. "Interesting," she murmured. "And how did you meet Eton?"

He told her, and she wasn't at all surprised because she'd seen Eton as that kind of guy. Although it might have been a business deal, more for information than anything, but she didn't tell Joe that. Besides, it still came from the same place, which was from Eton's heart.

"Well, let him check it out," she said. "Then we should be good to go."

"You're sure he is safe?"

"No," she said, "but I'm betting my life on it."

"Exactly," he said. "I guess that's why I called."

ETON SLIPPED OUT into the darkness, away from the house to take a good look around. No reason for anybody to be here bothering Joe, but that didn't mean that assholes didn't unite for a cause and usually the wrong one. With Sammy safely inside with Joe, Eton quickly swept around the outside area, checking the trees, looking all around the area to see if anybody was keeping an eye on him. Sammy had mentioned a stranger outside her house last night as well. But why?

Was that related to Annie's husband or was that something else completely? Because no doubt things could get confused when multiple issues arose. That Joe was here and that he'd received a threat and didn't want to go to work tonight was obvious. But, if he didn't go, that would also send off some alarms. They needed to avoid that as well.

Things were coming to a crunch, but Eton wasn't sure if any of the issues were connected to his case. That was a frustrating thing when you had a lot of different seemingly unconnected threats happening. Like now. But he felt a kinship with Joe, who was just trying to help out his family. He seems to have gotten caught in something that was particularly ugly.

Seeing absolutely nothing out of the ordinary outside, Eton made his way to the house and knocked on the door. It was opened immediately, and Joe stood there, shuffling from one foot to the other.

Eton gave him a reassuring smile. "Nothing that I saw out there."

A whisper of relief crossed his face, and his shoulders stiffened. "Didn't figure it was," he said. "Doesn't mean there isn't anything at the jobsite."

Eton nodded. "I'm still thinking about that."

"I have a suggestion," he said. "Why don't I come up with you tonight, and I'll take a look around myself."

"Oh, I can't ask you to do that," Joe protested.

"Yes, you can," Sammy said from the background. Joe turned to look at her, and she nodded encouragingly. "This is what he does," she said. "Let him see if he finds any issues or signs of anything funny."

Joe asked, "Could he also tell if anybody is using it for a safe drop or if it's a telecommunication center?"

She gazed at Eton, with a challenging look.

He nodded. "Yes, I probably could," he said, "but I'd have to ask why?"

"The boss's son is into that kind of stuff," Joe muttered.

"Of course he is. Give me five minutes to check out the rest of your house."

At that, Joe frowned. He looked at Sammy again.

She stepped forward and asked, "Why?"

"Because I want to make sure nobody unexpected entered the house," Eton said in exasperation. "I would have done it first. But I wanted to check out who was outside."

"Do you really think it's possible for somebody to have gotten in without him knowing?"

"Happens all the time," he said. "Do we want to argue about it or fix it?"

"If somebody is here or has been here, we need to know," she said. She turned to Joe, and, instead of trying to explain it to him in English, she gave it to him in his own language.

Joe immediately nodded his head and stepped back. They followed Eton as he went from room to room, and, although he didn't see anything, Eton found a window that had been tampered with.

He pointed it out to Joe, whose expression immediately changed to one of fear. He looked at Sammy.

Joe obviously trusted Sammy more than he did Eton. Which was understandable. "Is he sure he wants to go to that job tonight?" Eton asked.

"His grandson means a great deal to him," she said quietly.

"I get that, but something hinky is going on, and surely he can get another job around here."

"No, not really," she said, "not without having to go into a larger town, and he can't do that easily."

Eton didn't stop to worry about it because people said things all the time and yet found a way, but he saw Joe was pretty adamant about it.

"Okay then, I'm driving you home," Eton said to Sammy, "and I'll go with Joe up to the job."

"If you say so," she said, frowning.

"I'll finish checking the rest of the house first," Eton said, and, with that, he made a fast trip through the rest of Joe's house. Everything else was fine, but Eton also needed to set a couple traps to see if anybody opened things up while Joe was gone to work. And so Eton set a couple hairs on the window, pointed it out to Joe, and explained that—if somebody opened the window, and it wasn't Joe—he would know because that hair would be gone.

Joe immediately nodded his head, and then, with a look back at Sammy, Eton said, "Come on. Let's go."

"Joe will go on ahead of us," she said, as they all three left at the same time, Joe already in his car.

Eton nodded. "In that case, I want to get to the jobsite as soon as possible."

"You really think something's wrong?" she asked, as she got into his vehicle.

"How freaked out was Joe to you?"

"Very," she said quietly.

"Is he the kind who freaks out?"

"No," she said, "not at all."

"Exactly, so it is what it is."

"It just seems so wrong," she said.

"It does, but that doesn't make it wrong," he said. "Something is going on, and obviously somebody has gotten suspicious of Joe."

"Good enough," she said. "You can just drop me off at the driveway, and I'll walk back up to my place."

But he wouldn't listen, and he quickly deposited her at her front door. "Go inside and lock your door," he said. "I'll call and check in with you later, as soon as I sort out what's going on at Joe's job."

"Is it connected to what you're up to?"

"I don't know," he said. "So far, we keep going on wild goose chases."

She nodded and slammed the door shut, then he turned and headed out to the building site.

He parked just behind Joe, but so the other man could get out, if need be. As Eton walked in the adjoining building, he froze, then bolted into action. Joe was on the floor, blood pooling on the side of his skull from a head wound. Instincts firing, Eton quickly checked for a pulse, and, when he got that, he sent a message to Sammy to order an ambulance; then he sent a message to Garret, letting him know what was up. Eton hated to leave the old man as he was defenseless on the floor, but Eton gained absolutely no benefits by staying here with Joe if an intruder were still around.

Eton figured, when Joe arrived, he caught the intruder doing something. That pissed off Eton because he'd planned on getting here earlier too. Knowing that there would be chaos when the first responders arrived, he quickly searched the area, looking for an intruder. No vehicle had gone down the road because he'd been coming up the same road. He turned to look at the vehicles outside, wondering if the attacker had used one. So many of the buildings themselves were locked, so it was hard to get in. It would take precious time to get into most of them to check.

He stationed himself outside and quickly hit the hills, looking for anybody running away. Nobody could escape in the darkness quietly if they were in a hurry. The trouble was, it was quiet, as if somebody sat out there, hunkered down and waiting, knowing they would make too much noise and were holding off on making their escape. That worked for Eton because he had great nighttime vision, and, as far as he was concerned, this asshole was his. All Eton had to do was find him. As he searched through the darkness, he thought he heard a branch crack on the high-rise side. He slipped backward, circled around at a run, coming toward the spot to the west. Just as he was about to proceed on again, he thought he saw movement. He looked deeper, and, sure enough, a male was crouched among the brush.

He'd managed to stay hidden for a long time. Which also meant he probably had training and was most likely a pro. That would mean he was armed. Eton couldn't guarantee just how Joe had been attacked, but it didn't look like a bullet wound, unless it was just a graze. Either way, Joe was done here, and, after this, the company would have a hard time getting any security in place. Eton slipped a little bit lower into the underbrush, trying to stay as quiet as possible and under the radar. Finally the man stood and ever-so-slowly checked his watch, then turned as if to run away.

As he pivoted, he came up directly against Eton's right fist.

CHAPTER 8

T HE SIGHT OF the text from Eton paralyzed Sammy. She immediately phoned for assistance for Joe, but then she got another text, this one from Garret, saying he'd already contacted the ambulance. She stood here, staring at her phone, when Annie called. Trying to shift gears, she answered the phone. "Hey, are you okay?"

"I am," her friend said, "but you sound a bit rattled."

"Yeah, I definitely am," she said, "but it's okay. How are you doing? Any contact with your ex?"

"Well, he phoned today. I asked him about the tires, and he sounded honestly shocked."

"Do you believe him?"

"I don't know," she said. "I made it very clear that I'm not currently dating anybody, and, if he is pulling any shit like that, I would have the cops call him."

"What kind of reaction did he have?"

"Well, he was definitely interested in whether I was dating or not," Annie said, sounding weary. "But I still don't want to get back with him."

"Did you make that clear?"

"I'm not sure you *can* make that clear to him," she said. "He doesn't want to listen. He doesn't want to hear what I say. He wants to hear only the words he wants to hear."

"I get it," she said. "But still, maybe it will be the end of the shenanigans, if he doesn't think you're dating."

"What happens when I do date then?" Annie asked, worried. "Will he turn around and feel that way again?"

"It's possible," Sammy said.

"What are we supposed to do then?"

"I don't know. Give it some time, I guess."

"I did call my mom and told her, and she wants me to contact the lawyer and get some no-contact order against him."

"Well, you could," she said. "I just would hate to see anything escalate, if you are on peaceable terms with him right now."

"And yet, if he did it, how peaceable is it right now?" she asked, with a sad sigh.

"I hear you," she said. "You've got to do what you feel is best."

"Whatever that means," she said. "Listen though. Why are you so rattled?"

"Just some shit going down," she said. "The usual." She tried to keep her voice happy. It appeared to work because Annie was off again on another tangent.

"I'm thinking about moving," she said abruptly.

Sammy winced. "Why? You know how I feel about that," she said.

"I know, but you're the only one I'd miss from here," she said. "But honestly, after this, I don't want to be anywhere around here."

"Understandable. Where would you go?"

"I'm not exactly sure yet, but I have friends in Holland. I was thinking about visiting there for a while."

"Well, that's a surprise," she said. "When you're talking about moving, you're talking about really moving. I thought you just meant to a different house."

"Yeah, well, if you'll take the time and effort to do it, you might as well do it right," she said. "Right?"

"Yes," she said, trying to be encouraging. "Besides, it would give me a reason to come visit."

"True," she said. "You've got lots of local friends anyway, don't you?"

"I wouldn't say that," she said, "but I have to make some decisions regarding my father in the future anyway." She sighed. "So who knows what my plans may end up being?"

And this time, Annie stopped, suddenly subdued. "That's right," she said. "Our lives are changing, aren't they?"

"They definitely are," she said, "and it doesn't matter because we'll still be friends, whether we are sitting around the corner from each other or not."

"Right, that's what I was hoping you'd say," she said, with a half laugh.

"When are you looking at going?"

"Well, it really just came up from the conversation with my mother."

"Where is she living now?"

"Oh, she's in Amsterdam too right now."

"Living there?"

"She is doing a special study there. Something about the water levels with the sea levels rising," she said, "so she'll be there for a few years."

"Well, you know that sounds like a great reason to move there, at least for a few years anyway," she said. "You haven't spent much time with her."

"No, and it was her suggestion," she confessed.

"You don't need to feel bad about that," she said. "Go. If

I had a chance to spend time with my mother, you know I would do it in a heartbeat."

"Well, that's partly what I was first thinking about, you know? With your father and the shape he is in. Who knows how much longer I'll have my mother?" she said.

"Exactly, and it's important that you end up enjoying something in your life and taking the time that you have for each other," she said. "In a way, with my father's condition as it is, that reminds me every day that what time we have together is special and that it will be over one day. So instead of focusing on the future and missing out on the time we have now, I'm trying to make the most of it."

"Yeah, I think that is partly what I'm thinking right now. Something about the divorce, the tire slashing, just that whole nightmare," she said.

"You don't need to explain," Sammy said. "I understand. So when is your rent up?"

"Well, that's another thing," she said. "The landlord contacted me to see if I was staying long-term because he has a family member looking for a home."

"And he wants to give your rental to him, right?" she said, with an understanding nod. "Sometimes life is like that. It gives you these hints and these offers, then waits to see which way you'll bend."

"Well, the bend looks like a move," she said. "I'm just not sure what to do with all the stuff that's here."

"Ditch it," she said. "Most of it is secondhand stuff anyway, not like inherited from your family, right?" she said. "If you care about anything, have it shipped, but that's probably expensive, and you could replace nearly everything there."

"I know, but still I have to get rid of it somehow."

"Even better, sell it, or give it away," Sammy said. "Put a

'free, come get it' sign on it. Just be sure you've got anything you want to keep out of the way. Whatever you don't give away, you can have someone haul it to a secondhand store or maybe a charity bazaar or even a church or homeless shelter."

"Ha, I never thought of that," she said. "This is why I keep you around."

"It might be a good idea just from the standpoint of a new beginning."

"Yeah, *new*, indeed," she said. "And then what?"

"Hard to say, but be open to whatever comes."

At that, her friend rang off.

Sammy stared at the phone and placed it slowly on the counter. She realized it was the end of an era happening. It was sad, yet it was all happening at the same time. She would miss her friend, but she didn't have to make that absence huge. Just so much of Sammy's time and energy were spent with her father right now that Sammy hadn't had much time to spend with friends anyway. She could pick up with her friend later; at least she hoped to. But still her priority was her father.

As she sat here at the kitchen table, she'd forgotten to put on the teakettle. She'd come in to do just that but hadn't gotten any farther when her phone rang. With the kettle on now, she kept looking down at her phone, wondering what was happening with Eton. She wanted to find out, but, at the same time, if he was in the midst of some supersecret spy stuff, she didn't want to buzz his phone and distract him or, even worse, alert the enemy. She didn't think Garret was in the same boat, so she quickly sent him a text message, asking for an update.

The answer came back fast. **Nothing yet.**

She responded with a simple inquiry.**Joe?**

The ambulance is there.

She wondered about going up to see for herself, making sure Joe was okay, but almost immediately she got another text from Garret.

Don't go.

Frowning, she replied at once. **Are you psychic?**

No, but I've come to understand who you are from Eton. So I know that you care, but, in this case, I need you safe.

Why? She wrote back, still frowning.

Because Eton cares.

She stared at the message in shock and sat down again. **No, he doesn't.** She wrote, stunned at the thought.

But did she know that? Did she know anything about him at all? It just seemed so odd, all of it. But, at the same time, he was also fascinating. Just the thought of a guy like that being interested was enough to set her back a little bit and to cause her to rethink her strategy in life. She was okay to sit at home and do nothing when nothing else was on offer, but, when something else was right here, maybe her life needed some reconsideration. Maybe it wasn't just Annie who needed to do a complete switch. Certainly something to think about. Besides, it was early. It's not like Sammy knew Eton though.

But what she did know? She liked Eton. It was just stressful being in a scenario like this because she wasn't prepared to let her father be alone for any length of time in the next little while. She wasn't prepared to let him go at this stage. Or ever. Regardless he needed her, and that was her focus. But, at the same time, that small voice inside her said they didn't have to be mutually exclusive. She could have a friendship and even a relationship with somebody, while caring for her father in his golden years. She could be there for Dad without giving up everything else in life.

She frowned, wondering just how much of that part of her that always yearned to have that special relationship was just a devil's advocate, voicing any alternative opinion. Her father never understood why it hadn't happened, and maybe she'd never taken a swing at it because it seemed that the men out there were little boys instead, while what she wanted was a man secure in his world. There seemed to be a shortage of those around.

At that, she smiled, made her tea, and then walked into the living room to check on her father, not surprised to find him once again sleeping on the couch. She studied him with a soft look on her face. He had such an otherworldly look to him, almost as though he already had one foot in the grave. In that moment, she realized that part of the problem was that he was probably sticking around for her sake.

In many ways she imagined he may be ready to go to whatever came afterward. She'd been raised without religious beliefs, and her father was a bit of an agnostic. It would be interesting for him to discover the truths evermore. All of them. It was a journey each had to make alone, hoping they had made the right choice all these years before or even in their last minute of life here. In her case, she just wanted him to be happy and safe. She imagined it was likely the same for him.

Just then he opened his eyes, looked at her, and frowned. "Is there a problem?"

She shook her head. "No, not at all," she said quietly. "I was just wondering if I should wake you."

He yawned, nodded, and said, "I should probably just go to bed." Then he stopped, focused on her, and asked,

"How was the date?"

She didn't even bother trying to explain. "It was good, Dad."

He beamed. "Perfect," he said. "Let me know when the wedding is." Then he got up and stumbled toward his bed.

She just shook her head. "No wedding, Dad."

"There will be," he said. "I knew as soon as I heard that voice."

"Why is that?"

"Prayers were answered."

"You aren't religious," she said. "Nobody is answering your prayers."

"That's what you think," he said. "I've been asking your mother for help forever."

ETON STARED DOWN at the unconscious man at his feet on the forest floor. He'd already texted an update to Garret and had sent a photo image of the man's face, but, in this poor light, the flash bleached out his features, so Eton hoped it was good enough. He sent Garret a message, asking him to check with Ice as well.

On it, Garret replied. **Anything else down in the buildings?**

Ambulance and police are there.

Anonymous caller, huh?

Must have been a Good Samaritan who called it in.

Eton smiled, as he hung up. He'd already checked the man in the trees in front of him for identification but found nothing. He'd taken off his shoes and socks, then checked every inch of his clothing for anything that would identify him. He even had his shirt off, looking for tattoos. But found nothing. The man groaned; suddenly his eyes flashed open, and he jolted, tried to come up, but no way he was getting up since his ankles were tied together and so were his hands. He glared at Eton and swore a blue streak, but in a language that Eton didn't know. He pulled out his phone and put it on Translate, with a special app that a friend of his had developed. Immediately the curse words turned into English. The spoken language was identified as an Italian dialect. When the man ran out of insults, Eton waited, but his prisoner had laid back down again and said, "Fuck you."

"Well, that I understand," he said, "but, if you're the guy who hit old Joe on the head, you have a maker to meet who is also pretty likely to say that to you too."

The guy stared at him, then spoke in English. "I don't know what you're talking about."

"You were hiding in the trees, like a criminal," Eton said, "while the old man is down there, working to raise money for surgery that his grandson needs. Meanwhile, you are being an absolute asshole and hitting him over the head."

"Maybe I didn't do it," he said.

"Maybe you did," Eton said. "So, I'm asking you once, and I won't ask again. What are you doing up here?"

"I could ask you the same question."

"But you don't know anything about me," he said.

"I know that you're one of Bullard's men and that your life is marked."

"You're not the first person to tell me that," he said, "but I still don't know why. So unless you have any answers to that question, you really are of no use to us."

"What will you do then? Kill me?"

"Well, I could," he said. "You're just the dregs of society, aren't you? It's not like anybody needs you."

"Same as you," he said. "I'm just getting paid to take you out."

"Well, apparently they didn't pay enough to get good help," he said, "because you're not taking me out, not in the situation you're in," Eton said, with a half smirk.

"You're just some fancy asshole," he said, "but you're nothing special."

"I don't have to be special," Eton said "because you're nothing. Besides, you're my prisoner now." He raised the man to his feet. "Now, start walking." He led him cross-country. Slowly. The guy's feet were bound, so he was taking baby steps.

"Where are we going?" he asked.

"I've got a friend waiting," he said.

"And I don't believe that," the man said.

"I don't give a shit if you believe me or not," Eton replied.

"Why are you taking me anywhere?"

"Because I want to. We already went over this," he said. "Besides, you're just an asshole. What do I care if you believe me or not?"

"Maybe," he said, "maybe not. Maybe there is a method to my madness."

"You hit an unarmed senior citizen," he said, "just because you were directed to, I presume."

"Maybe he was too nosy. Maybe he came where nobody goes, saw me there, and tried to stop me. Maybe he was trying to play the hero. Maybe I had no choice, and I had to knock him out. Or maybe I didn't do it at all."

"Shut up, asshole. You could have stopped him without hurting him, but you like to hurt people," he said.

"I'll enjoy hurting you," he snapped.

At that, Eton elbowed him hard across the head.

"See? You're just the same as I am."

"No, I'm not. I'm nothing like you," he said. He frowned when he got a text from Garret. He picked up the phone and called him. "I'm bringing him in to see if we can get some answers."

"What about the vehicle?"

"I'll truss him up, leave him in the trunk, and bring him over to you," he said.

"Good enough," he said. "Watch your back."

That was a good reminder, and, as he put away his phone, he wondered if this guy was working alone. "Where is your partner anyway?"

"Who says I've got one?" he snapped. "If you've got a partner, you've got to share the wages."

"Ah, so you were just hired to take me out," he said. "That's not too smart of you to come alone."

"Smart enough to get paid for it," he said. And he started to laugh. "You don't know jack shit, do you?"

"Well, one of us doesn't," Eton said. "It'd be nice if you'd give us some answers."

"Won't happen."

"Was that written into the contract?"

"What?"

"Your silence?" Eton asked.

"Everybody knows, with this guy, that if you don't keep quiet, you're dead," he said.

"What do you mean?" Eton said. "Because everybody knows that whoever works for this guy is dead regardless. We've been following his tracks all the way along, and he is cleaning up. Nobody is left alive."

"That's not true," his captive said hotly.

"Yeah, it is, but I don't give a shit if you believe me or

not," he said. At the car, he unlocked it, kept the keys in his pocket, and standing the captive at the end of vehicle, grateful that all the cops and the ambulance were gone, quickly knocked his prisoner on his head and lowered him into the trunk. Then he snapped it closed, walked to the driver's side door, sat down in the seat, and called Garret. "I'm on the way back."

"Okay, but remember. There could be a second one."

"So, if you can, keep track as I come up," he said, "because I'm on my way now."

"See you in five."

Eton sat, with the door open, taking another look around. As he turned on the engine with one hand and had his other hand on the car door to shut it, the car exploded. Eton was blasted through the open door, hitting the ground a good ten feet away. He stayed there, stunned, and realized the blast had come from the trunk, where his prisoner was. The trunk had been blown open, but it was obvious his prisoner was dead. He stood up, backing away from the inferno, then pulled out his phone and quickly told Garret what had happened.

"Goddammit," Garret snapped. "Do you think he did it?"

"I don't know," he said, "I have no fucking idea at the moment."

"I suggest you get out of there," he said. "I'll contact Ice to see if she can do anything about the mess. And get an update on the search."

"Not a whole lot to clean up. He'll burn up as the fire eventually works its way through him, but it's bullshit," he said. "We needed answers."

"Maybe, but remember that part about watch out for his partner? Because it sure looks like he has one onsite."

CHAPTER 9

S AMMY HEARD THE explosion from inside her bedroom. Standing up, she raced outside to the balcony and turned to find out whatever had caused it. In the distance, toward the condo development where Joe worked, she saw what she thought was fire. She quickly phoned the number that had texted her, and Garret answered. "Is he okay?" she asked.

"Not as good as he should be," Garret said, his voice calm and reassuring. "His car was blown up."

She gasped in horror.

"Unfortunately, along with the guy he found. The guy is dead, but Eton is okay."

"Jesus Christ," she whispered.

"I know. It was another close one."

"*Another* close one?" she said in an ominous tone of voice.

"Yeah," he said clearly. "We are doing this for a reason. We have people out there who are after us, and we don't know why."

"That's terrible," she said. "You'll spend your whole lives looking over your shoulders."

"Which is why Eton generally doesn't get into relationships," he said gently. "Why we're always afraid of somebody close to us getting hurt."

"But then," she thought about that and said, "it's just really sad because he's alone his whole life. And you."

"And that's the reason why it's hard to get committed because he goes back and forth, considering his options, because he cares, but he can't afford to care."

"What about when this is over?"

"Well, that's the hope," he said. "We just aren't there yet."

"Well, find the bastard," she said, "because I have no intention of walking away."

Garret burst out laughing. "Well, I hear you," he said, "and I'm glad too because Eton deserves to have somebody who cares that much."

"Well, I do care. I don't know how much, and I sure as hell didn't need the explosion to happen to remind me. I was just thinking about the changes I need to make in my world as it is."

"Why is that?"

"Because of my father," she said. "It won't be too much longer for him."

"I'm sorry," he replied. "You're lucky you have this time with him."

"That's what I was just thinking. Go help Eton," she said and hung up. She sat here, almost frozen, as she tried to figure out what she was supposed to do. Just so many truths were coming home to her, and she didn't know quite how to take it. She didn't really have enough interactions to know who Eton really was, but it was horrible that he would be alone because people were targeting him and his team.

She wanted the whole story from him but knew it would require a little more on her part to get it. He was a good man, and she just hoped that he wasn't hurt from any of this. It all sucked. But she would do what she could to make his life a little bit easier, the same as she was for her father. She just wasn't sure how. She went downstairs to the kitchen to make a cup of tea, but, when her phone rang a few minutes later, she snatched it up to see Eton was calling. "How are you?" she asked in a rush.

"I'm fine," he said, but his voice was tired. "Just a surprise ending to the evening."

"I'm glad you found Joe," she said. "Where are you now?" she asked tersely.

"I'm back at the chalet," he said. "Garret told me that you called."

"Yes." She took a slow deep breath, pinching the bridge of her nose. "I was worried when I heard that blast. I knew it would be you."

He chuckled. "Well, I managed to escape another one," he murmured.

"That's not funny," she said. "Garret told me about the lifestyle you live."

"Well, believe it or not, this isn't normal," he said. "An awful lot of the time, things merely roll along, and we don't have danger or anything like this."

"Good," she said, "because this is unnerving. You'll have to stop it."

"Oh, I will, will I?" She heard a smile in his voice. "And why is that?"

"Because I can't keep up a relationship if I have all that stuff to deal with at the same time too. So you'll just have to find a way around it."

"Interesting," he murmured.

"Yes."

"Relationship?"

"Yes," she said, "and don't tell me that you're not interested because I know you are."

"Definitely interested," he said briskly. "Which is another reason why I want to make sure you stay safe."

"I'm safe at the moment. Am I not likely to be?"

"I don't think there's a direct issue with you," he said. "They are after me and Garret and the rest of our team."

"So why did they go after Joe?" she asked. "That makes no sense to me."

"No, it doesn't to me either," he said. "It sounds like Joe found them doing something that they didn't want him to know about."

"Have you talked to him?"

"He's still unconscious," Eton said. "We just got a report on his condition."

"Great," she said in exasperation. "Do you do anything but wait for information to come through?"

"Unfortunately that is a pretty regular state in our world," he said.

"It sucks," she announced ceremoniously.

"It does, indeed," he said, but a smile was in his voice, and she had to admit a smile was in hers too.

"After—well, my father—I've decided I'll move," she said abruptly.

He froze and asked, "Where to?"

"I'm not sure yet," she said, "but I've spent a lot of my life here. And I know the last few years, it's basically only been because he's failing," she said, "and I didn't want to leave him alone. But that doesn't have to be what I do afterward."

"No," he said, "it doesn't. And I'm sure he would want you to live the life that you want to live, instead of just looking after him."

"I won't leave him until it's over," she said quietly.

"Of course not," he said. "He's your father, and you obviously love him very dearly."

"I do," she said. "It's just been the two of us since my mother passed, and that's been quite a few years now," she said.

"And again, enjoy the time you have with him because it can be over all too soon," he said.

"As the bomb going off in the car demonstrated so well," she said in exasperation. He chuckled at that. "Will you be safe tonight?" she asked him.

"I think so. I'll take a power nap and grab a few hours of rest, and then we'll be back to tracking as much as we can find out about this guy."

"He's already dead, so what will that do for you?"

"He'll lead us to somebody," he said. "Somebody else nearby must have known that I had him. Otherwise, why set off a bomb in the car? Unless of course it was on him, but I searched him from top to bottom," he said. "He didn't have anything on him."

"Right, so somebody saw you grab him and took the opportunity to set a detonator on the vehicle. Pretty ballsy."

"It is, isn't it?" he said, with a smile. "And something that we aren't exactly used to. These guys have a lot of confidence in what they're doing, but, in this case, I think they were also desperate to make sure they got something taken care of and done."

"Got it," she said. "Go to sleep. You need it." And she hung up on him. She turned around to see her father leaning against the kitchen wall.

"I'm sorry," he said abruptly.

She frowned and walked closer. "For what, Dad?"

"I'm stopping you from living your life."

"Oh, no, you don't," she said. "You won't pull that one on me. I'm exactly where I want to be."

"Too late," he said, "but I have to admit to being selfishly delighted."

She smiled, then reached out and kissed him gently. "It is what it is, Dad."

"But what I really want is for you to be happy and settled," he fretted. "And that won't happen while you are looking after your old man."

"I'm looking after you because I want to," she said, "not because I have to."

"But you would say that," he said, "because you are a beautiful person."

"And you are my father. I love you and don't want anything less than you having somebody at your side for the rest of your life."

"What if it takes years and years?" he said, straightening up with a frown. "I've never even looked for any treatment. I just knew I was failing. I wasn't too bothered about it because it was comfortable."

"What are you saying?"

"I don't know," he said, staring off in the distance. "Maybe I can improve some of this in some way. I don't know. I just didn't want to go through the tests."

"So, what's changed?"

He slid a glance her way. "You."

"I love that you would do this for me because I want all the time I can have with you. But it seemed to me that you were interested in meeting up with Mom in some way, right? In whatever your version of the hereinafter looks like. I want you happy with your decision. I don't want you doing something that has you living less of a life here with me," she said.

He chuckled. "I'm not trying to, but there is no doubt that I would like to see you happy and settled, and, if there happens to be a man in your world, then maybe I need to take another look at whether more can be done for me. Maybe I can get a few more years out of it, while you and this fella get more serious."

"You should get all the years available for you," she said. "As long as you are happy here."

He reached over, tapped her gently on the chin, and said, "But that is what you are doing for me."

"And again," she said, tears coming to her eyes, "I want whatever time we have together to be the best time."

"It is." He opened his arms, and she stepped into them.

"You always said that you didn't want to go through all the tests and drug treatments."

"And the doctor did make it seem like he couldn't do a whole lot for me," he said, "but I never did go for a second opinion, and maybe I should have. I just didn't care, up until now."

"And was that because of Mom?"

"Probably," he said, with half a smile. "But that's also very selfish on my part."

"No, Dad, you have to do whatever is right for you," she said, with a smile. "I wouldn't want anything less."

"I get it," he said, "but an awful lot is out there for you in this world, and I don't want you stuck here, looking after me."

She frowned, not liking that tone. "Stop it," she ordered. "It's been a stressful night. I can't take too much more of this."

"I know," he said. "You should go to bed."

"I will," she said.

And he smiled and nodded. "Well then, I'm back to bed too. I do know that I'm always tired, and I need rest."

"Are you sure they couldn't do anything?"

"Like I said, the doc said there wasn't, but did he mean it? I don't know."

She frowned, as he walked away, because of course she wanted him to live, but she'd always gotten the feeling that he didn't want to go through whatever was necessary in order to make that living happen—maybe because the quality of living wasn't there? Even now, she knew he wasn't happy with his poor quality of life. But she loved him and was willing to stand by his side, no matter what.

After he headed off to bed, she straightened up the kitchen. Staring out the window over the kitchen sink, she whispered, "Stay safe, Eton." And she headed off to bed. She could only hope that they would get through this without any trouble, but it was already looking like a long shot.

ETON TOSSED DOWN the phone and walked into the kitchen, where the coffee was dripping. He grabbed a cup before it was done and turned to lean against the counter. He reached up and rubbed his head.

"You look like shit," Garret said cheerfully.

"You think?"

"A shower would make you feel better."

"I'm just fueling up before I head back in about an hour," he said. "Somebody saw me. Somebody was watching me, and I didn't see them, and that pisses me off."

"What are the chances that whoever was watching you is the one who took out Joe?"

"It's possible, but it seems like somebody is always watching the operatives in this business, just like Tristan got taken out too."

"And it could be the same guy," he said. "We don't have any way of knowing."

"No, but we should have," he said. "I checked everything that was on my prisoner but found nothing. I took photos of his chest, looking for existing or removed tattoos. There was nothing," he said. "And again that pisses me off."

"But that doesn't mean that we don't get something on facial recognition."

"I sure hope so," Eton said, "because, so far, we are not getting anywhere."

"We've only been here a couple days," Garret said, "so hold tight. We're getting there."

"Bullshit," he said forcibly. "We're getting nowhere." He slammed down his cup of coffee and walked out onto the balcony, staring in the direction of the building complex. Garret came out beside him. They stood in silence for a few minutes. Finally Eton spoke. "I almost died again tonight."

"Makes you rethink things, doesn't it?" Garret said. "Waking up from that coma wasn't much fun. Finding out Bullard was missing and presumed dead was a hard way to remember that life is all about living. And pretty damn soon we are done with that part of our lives and are into dying already."

"It's a tough road right now."

"Only because you're frustrated at having nowhere to turn. You want a target, and I can't give you one."

"I know," he said, stretching out his tight shoulders.

"What about the rest of the team?"

"They finished running down everybody in Tristan's world, and nothing is pointing anywhere but here. We thought this was the best tangent early on, so we took it. And we appear to be right."

"Are we though?" Eton asked. "It could be that we're just up against other issues here. Shit is going on all around the world," he said. "This one could be just more of the same."

"Are you thinking about Sammy right now?"

"Sammy and her girlfriend, yeah," Eton said.

"Well, the ex could be involved in that slashing-tires deal," Garret said. "I got the impression that Sammy is ready to leave when this is over."

"She said something about it tonight. After her father's gone."

"Is he that bad?"

"I don't know," Eton said. "Sounds like it."

"Something we have to consider though," Garret said.

"No, we don't," Eton said, swearing. "I can't bring her into my world with this." He swung his arms out wide. "No bloody way."

"That's true, so we have to solve this so we can open the pathway for something more."

Eton gave a startled laugh. "A serious relationship has never been my focus. You know that."

"I know, but that doesn't mean it shouldn't be though."

"Maybe, but we're not getting anywhere here, so I can't even think about one," Eton said.

"Now you're back to being negative again," Garret said. "Come on. Let's take a look at something I did find today."

"And what was that?"

"I pulled all the cell phones registered to anybody in that local area around the townhomes," he said, "and we've got some interesting patterns happening."

Interested in spite of himself, Eton turned and looked at him. "Like *interesting*, interesting?"

"Oh, yeah, very interesting."

"Will it lead to this dead asshole that we've got?"

"Depends what we get for an ID on him. Maybe," he said.

Just then Eton's phone rang. He pulled it out and said, "Ice, I hope you've got something for us."

"And I hope your ass was handed to you for that little stunt," she said in exasperation. "Do you know you could have been killed?"

"Thanks, *Mom*," he said in a mocking voice.

She laughed. "Go ahead. Make me feel like shit for worrying about your ass," she said. "But you had to know there was likely a partner, and that should have been a given from the beginning."

"It was," he said, "but I was free and clear, just bringing my prisoner back here."

"Why? Where was your partner?"

He sucked in his breath at that and looked at Garret.

Garret snatched the phone from his hand. "He's been trying to keep me grounded," Garret said. "Hi, Ice."

It was her turn to gasp. "Garret?"

"Yeah," he said. "Wish I could have a hug right about now."

"Oh, my God, no wonder Eton went alone."

"I'm fine," Garret said. "Everybody needs to stop treating me like an invalid."

"They'll stop treating you that way if you weren't acting

that way," she said, her tone crisp.

"Ouch," he said. "That's not fair anyway, since they won't let me get any action."

"That's because they care," she said.

"I do too," he said. "Now enough of this taking care of me. I'm here to help take care of Eton."

"Well, you need to do a better job of it," she said in a dry voice.

"After tonight, you're not kidding," he said. "Bullshit, isn't it? Did you have a reason for calling?" Garret put the phone on Speaker and handed it back to Eton.

"Yeah, we've got an ID on your dead guy."

"Good, who is he?"

"Harry Gann, normally operates out of Italy, so Switzerland isn't much of a stretch for him."

"Who does he normally work for?"

"Private," she said, "but we've got his bank accounts, so we're tracking the money. He was paid fifty thousand last week."

"Wow. Wonder if that was a two-for-one deal or just for me," Eton said. "I'm flattered."

Whereas Garret laughed and said, "I'm insulted."

"Well, we don't know exactly what the scope of the job was or whether he had to split that money either, so keep your shirts on. I'm sending you the information we've pulled, and you need to look for a partner. He often hangs around with another guy, an older guy. We are wondering if they work together or if they're family. I've sent you a photo of him too."

"I'll take a look. I'll call you back if I have anything," Eton said, as Garret walked over to the laptop and brought up the email, then clicked on the photo.

"What about him? Do you recognize this guy?" Garret asked Eton.

Eton walked over to join Garret and started swearing.

"What? Who is he?" Garret asked.

"That's the guy I found hurt. That's Joe," he said.

Garret stared at Eton. "Seriously?"

"Yes, and that means it was a setup from the beginning," Eton said and started cursing heavily. He picked up the phone, called Ice back, and explained what they knew about the partner.

"Oh no, now that's a very interesting tidbit," she murmured. "Sucks too. But it looks like Joe was played."

"But by who?" Eton said. "Was it a coincidence, or was this a long-term setup?"

"I don't know, but you better check out the girlfriend too."

"That's bullshit," Eton said. "She doesn't have anything to do with this."

"No, she probably doesn't, but we didn't think Joe did either."

"On the other hand," Eton said, calming down, "Joe is in the hospital and still unconscious."

"What do you want to do?" Ice said.

"I want him to stay there, until I have a chance to bust his chops for this," he said. "And then I want to know who the hell is hiring everybody and to find out who Joe can lead us to."

"That's an interesting possibility," she said. "I'm contacting the hospital right now."

"Do you think they'll hold him for you?"

"I'll let you know." And she hung up.

"Damn," Eton said. "How the hell is that possible? Do

you think she knew?"

"Who?" But Garret knew who he meant.

"Sammy, who else?" Eton said.

"No, I don't think so," Garret said.

But, as Eton sat here, he wondered. "I think I need to pay her a visit. Phone calls only tell you so much," he said. "And, if she did have something to do with this shit, you can bet that I want to find out what else she might know," he said. He got up and headed out the door.

"Don't you want to call ahead or to take a shower first?"

"No, I'll pass on that right now," he said. "If she had anything to do with it, she needs to see a little bit of the destruction she caused."

And, with that, he tore out of there. He walked out front to Joe's vehicle, since Eton had taken it after his own had blown up and after Joe had been taken away in the ambulance. He hopped into Joe's car and headed down the road to the turn off where Sammy's house was. When he got there, he could feel his temper spiking even further. He didn't want to go in there furious at her, but it was hard to believe that she hadn't known something.

It wasn't fair to blame her just because he was angry at himself for being a sap, taken in by an old man with a story. Eton wanted to believe she hadn't had a clue, but a part of him hadn't learned to trust very easily. As he drove up to her house and knocked on the door, he wondered if he was a fool for being here. Was he just using anger as an excuse to come visit? Because that would really suck too.

But, when she opened the door, and her face shone with joy, he realized he was in deeper shit than he thought because that's exactly what he was here for. He opened his arms, and she ran into them. He closed them around her and held her tight.

"Come in. Come in," she whispered, when she could.

He shook his head. "I need to go home and have a shower," he said, "but we've had a rather ugly turn in the case, and I wanted to know if you had any insights."

She looked up, frowned at him. "What ugly turn?"

He frowned too, looked at her seriously, and shifted, so he saw her face in the light. "We got an ID on the man blown up in my trunk." He gave her the name, and she shrugged and said, "I don't know him, at least not the name."

"Here's the kicker. Somebody he works with a lot or who might be family of is Joe Chronie."

She stared at him, and her jaw dropped, and then he realized she truly didn't know. "Joe?"

He nodded grimly.

"As in *Joe*, Joe? The one in the hospital right now?"

"Yes, that one."

She shook her head. "Oh, my God, did he set you up? No, it couldn't have been him…"

"That's what I'm trying to figure out," he said. "I survived, but I'm not sure I was supposed to. So now I'm not sure who might have attacked him, but I know he didn't do it to himself."

She reached out and scrubbed her face. "This is so bizarre," she said. "Who would have thought?"

"Right. Just so much to figure out," he said, "but I wanted to know if you know anything about Joe's regular activities."

"I know he travels a lot," she said, "for odd jobs, as I understand it, and I've always known him as a strong family man."

"What does he have for family?"

"Two sons," she said. "One is married, with the grand-son who's in trouble."

"And the other one?"

She frowned. "I don't think I've ever heard much about him," she admitted. "I want to think that maybe he's adopted or something."

"That's the problem," he said. "It sounds like that one might be the one who just died."

"If it is, that would just break Joe," she whispered, her hand going to her mouth.

"True, but considering I was probably meant to die in that vehicle with Gann, I'm hoping that, if we go to the hospital and talk to Joe, I'll get some answers."

She nodded immediately. "Please talk to him first," she said. "Don't go in there accusing him or anything. Whatever he has done, he's done for love of family."

"Yeah, but that love of family can kill people too," he said.

"Apparently," she whispered. "I just can't believe it." She looked up at him. "And take a shower first. Please. You are scary enough without looking like you just survived a bombing."

He chuckled. "Garret told me to get a shower before I came here, but I didn't want to wait."

She smiled. "I'm glad you didn't," she said. "I've been so worried about you."

He looked down and noted she was in pajamas. "Did I get you out of bed?"

"I was sitting in the darkness, staring at the night around me, trying to figure out what to do with my life," she said.

"Do you have to make any decisions tonight?"

"No," she said. "But sometimes, just because you don't have to make them, decisions can be easier to make right now, instead of in a panic."

"Well, that was confusing," he said, with a smile, "but I think I understand."

"I think you do," she said. He turned to walk away, and she called out, "Who will tell Joe about his son?"

"I'm not sure the relationship has been very public," he said, "and I'm not even positive about the familial connection yet, so we'll have to verify. It might end up being me telling Joe," he admitted.

She winced at that. "That won't be easy."

"No, but it's about the best way for me to get the answers I need."

"Go easy on him," she said softly.

He stopped, looked at her, and said, "I will, if I can, but I've had just about enough attempts on my life. I'd probably be dead now, if my car door hadn't been open. And Garret was blown out of the sky over the ocean. I'm all out of patience."

"Okay," she whispered, and, as he walked away, he heard her whispering to the darkness.

"God help us all."

His heart felt the exact same sentiments.

CHAPTER 10

S AMMY WATCHED ETON go but with foreboding in her heart. She really wanted him to go easy on Joe, but she also understood that she was speaking as someone who had known Joe for a long time. Even though it might be a terrible idea, she felt like she should go with Eton. As soon as she closed the front door, she swore at herself for not offering to join him. She brought out her phone and texted him. **Come back and get me**, she ordered, as she ran to get changed out of her pajamas.

Instead her phone rang. "Why?" he asked. "I'm already down around the corner."

"I think you should come back. My being there will make it easier for Joe to talk to us."

"How well do you know him?"

"I've known him for years," she said. "I understand why he's done this."

"So do I," he said, "but it doesn't change anything."

"No, maybe not," she said, "but I still think I should be there."

"It could be dangerous."

"In what way?" she asked.

"It's possible that somebody will go after him. That's been a pattern, and that's why we've had trouble getting any information."

"Maybe," she said, "but that's not the issue right now."

"Damn it," he muttered. "I don't like it, Sammy."

"I don't care if you like it or not," she said, being as forceful as she could. "This needs to happen."

"And if I don't agree?"

She laughed. "Then I'll drive myself and do my very best to get in the way."

He started to swear.

She chuckled. "Don't you know when it's time to give in?" she asked.

"I know when it's time," he said, "but this is hardly it."

"It's definitely it," she snapped.

"Then get the hell out the door," he groused.

She opened the door, surprised to see him sitting in the vehicle, waiting for her. "Wow," she said, as she arrived at the car door, still talking on the phone. "I didn't realize you were already here."

"How could you?" he said. "You were too busy giving me hell."

She smiled at him, as she put away her phone and got into the vehicle. "There are times," she said, "when that's what needs to happen."

"Maybe so," he said, "but I don't want to get you into more danger."

"*More* danger?"

"Come on. You've got to know that anybody associated with me will be exposed to trouble. And I don't want that to happen. I don't want you to get hurt because of me."

"Well, in that case," she said, "if I keep close to you, you have to look after me anyway. If I'm here without you, and somebody attacks, then you won't be there to help me." He just shot her a hard look. She smiled, touched his cheek, and said, "Deal with it." He just shook his head. "Wow, you're not used to people pushing back, are you?"

"No, I'm totally used to people pushing back," he said. "My team and I discuss things back and forth all the time, and sometimes it can get heated, but rarely do I get outright resistance."

"Well, if you would have taken the hint and said something I wanted to hear," she said, "you wouldn't have this time either."

He burst out laughing at that. "Do you think life is that easy?" He asked the question sincerely, genuinely curious if she really thought that.

"Absolutely," she said. "Are you telling me that it isn't?"

"Yes. Life certainly isn't that easy. And I'm definitely not."

"No, you're not," she said. "You're a good guy, Eton, but I need to be there when you talk with Joe."

"I hope you're right," he said, "because it could be putting you in a bad spot."

"Like I said, in that case, the safest place for me is at your side."

He didn't say anything to that.

She looked over and said, "No argument?"

"No," he said, "in this instance, I don't have an argument that works."

"Good," she said and settled back.

"What about your friend? Annie, is it?"

"Yeah. She says she's moving to Amsterdam, to the Netherlands," she corrected herself. "I'm not too sure how quickly, but I suspect it will be sooner than I'd thought it would be."

"And why is that?"

"I think she's a little afraid of her ex or whoever is causing her problems, so she wants to just get up and leave."

"How fast can she go?"

"Pretty fast, I think," she said. "I talked to her earlier today, but I haven't heard from her since. So I think her discussion on this is over, and now she's taking action."

"You're expecting her to leave soon? Like, just get up and go?"

"I'm wondering about it, yes," she said. "I'm not too sure." As she thought about it, she replayed the phone call in her head. "You know what? I'm not sure why, but I have a funny feeling she might have already left." She pulled out her phone and dialed her friend.

When Annie picked up, Sammy said, "Hey, when are you planning on leaving?" After an awkward hesitation, she said, "You left already, didn't you?"

"I talked to Jorge. He confessed to slashing our tires. He even followed me to your house that night, to see where I was going. He said he was sorry, but ... I didn't think I could stay close by and not worry about what he'd do next. He was mad at you for still having me in your life, when he'd lost me. Not to mention he was watching both of our houses. He said he wouldn't do it again and begged me to still talk to him. But, after that call, I couldn't think of anything else but getting a long way away from him. Once I got it into my mind," she said, "I just couldn't stop thinking about it, and it seemed like the best idea."

"Got it," she said. "I'd like to have seen you beforehand."

"Well, we just spent time together," she said, with a smile in her voice. "Besides, you'll come and visit me, won't you?"

"Of course," she said. "It's just weird to know that you've gone already."

"I can't explain it except to tell you these past few days have been very difficult for me."

"That answer works," she said. "We all have to do what we need to do to stay safe." And, with that, she hung up the phone and looked at him.

He nodded. "I hear you," he said. "Times are changing."

"Very much so and that's an awkward thing. I'm not sure I really want to think about it."

"Got it, but, at the same time, we don't have a whole lot of choice, do we?"

"Maybe not, but it still feels weird."

"Not much to do but deal with it, huh?"

"Yep. Not a whole lot of choice," she murmured.

They were only a few minutes away from the hospital now.

"What tact will you use to get in to see him?"

He looked at her, smiled, and said, "I thought I'd be his son."

"Ouch," she said. "When he finds out it's you, and the news that you—oh, God."

"That's what you will be there to help me with," he said.

"What help will I give you?"

"Hopefully, whatever we need," he said, "because I need answers, no matter how they happen."

"Got it," she said, "but it's all still a bit weird."

"Unfortunately sometimes we have to do things like this."

"I guess."

When he pulled into the parking lot, she said, "I'm surprised to find it as empty as it is."

"It's evening," he said, "and late at that."

"Yeah. I'm afraid they won't let us in."

"Back to that immediate family member again, remember?"

She frowned, but, as he walked through the reception and found nobody there, he looked around.

"Someone should be here soon," she said encouragingly.

He nodded, flipped around the reception book.

"Someone's coming," she said.

Just then he heard the footsteps, so he turned the book back around again, so nobody would know. When the receptionist arrived, she talked to Sammy instead of Eton, calling her by name, speaking in their native tongue. Very quickly they found out where Joe was. With a smile of thanks, she turned and headed to the elevators.

"See? That was easy," he murmured.

She shook her head. "I don't like lying."

"Doesn't matter," he said. "Sometimes we have to do what we have to do."

And his words brought absolutely no argument from her. "Doesn't mean I have to like it though."

"Of course not. Let's go get some answers from Joe, so we have an idea of why he had to sell his soul."

"I wish you wouldn't put it that way."

"How would you like me to put it?" he asked, his voice hard.

She glanced at him. "Like somebody in a hard spot who had no choice."

"And maybe you're right," he said, "and maybe you just want him to be a nice person and to not deal with reality."

When they came to the door of Joe's room, she stopped Eton, frowned at him, and asked, "You'll be nice, right?"

He gave her a look.

She shrugged, knocked on the door, and, hearing a voice inside, she pushed it open and entered.

JOE'S FACE HAD been lit with a happy surprise at seeing her, but it turned to fear when Eton stepped in behind her. Eton stood in the doorway, trying not to crowd the man, who looked like he was about to explode. When it seemed like he had calmed down a bit, Eton asked, "Do you want to explain why you tried to get me killed?"

Joe stared at Eton in consternation, but immediately Sammy stepped forward and talked to him in his native tongue. Eton understood just enough to know that Joe didn't want to talk.

She came closer to Eton and whispered, "I don't want to be the one who tells him."

"Joe," Eton said, looking at him. "I know your son was in the middle of all this. Unfortunately the people who did this to you killed Harry tonight."

Joe stared at Eton in shock. He looked at Sammy, back at Eton, then shook his head. "No, no, he was working with him."

"But Harry failed," Eton said quietly. "Anybody who fails in that world doesn't survive another day."

"He didn't fail," Joe said. "We got you there."

"Is that why you helped him? Because otherwise, something like this would happen?"

Immediately Joe's head nodded. "They said that nothing would happen if we got you there."

"Well, something did happen. They blew up my vehicle, and your son was in there with me," he said.

"No, no, no, the bomb was for you, not for him."

"No, Joe," she said smoothly. "They detonated the bomb remotely, and they would have known Harry was inside."

"They were getting rid of a thread they didn't want to deal with," Eton said.

Joe looked at her with tears welling up in his eyes; then he sank back and started to cry. She reached over, grabbed his hand, and said, "I'm sorry," she said. "I'm really very sorry."

He tried hard to speak, and then he just gave up.

Eton leaned against the door and waited, wondering how long to give Joe to regain his composure. Finally, after a few moments, Joe used the sheet to wipe off his face.

Sammy gently but firmly took the lead. "Joe, we need to know who was involved in this," she said. "Obviously you turned Eton here over to the bad guys, and I want to believe that you had a good reason for it, but the bottom line is that you have now suffered a loss, and Eton is still alive. He is trying to save his own life and that of his team. They're all being targeted," she murmured.

He just stared at her and shook his head.

She nodded. "Yes, we need to know what's going on."

Joe looked at Eton, and the fear was back.

Eton asked him, "You think something will happen to you now?"

Joe pursed his lips, as he thought about it. "It's possible."

Eton stood with his arms across his chest, making no move to leave, until he got the answers he wanted. He looked at Joe and said, "You set me up and prepared to have me killed, for whatever reason you'd reconciled in your mind," he said. "Now your son is dead, and you've been attacked, and you yourself are likely the next target. I've always been a target, but this is new for you. What will you do about it? Save your life so you have a chance to help this other family of yours? Or was that all BS too?" he asked him, with absolutely no attempt to lighten the harshness of his voice.

He'd leave it to Sammy to try to soften this, to further explain. But, from the look on Joe's face, no more explanation was needed.

Then Joe rushed to speak, once again breaking back into the thick dialect that he and Sammy seemed to be natural at. Finally, when Joe fell silent, Sammy turned to Eton. "They offered a large amount of money. Enough to cover the surgery and all the equipment needed for his grandson."

She gave Eton a gentle smile. "Like I said, there is no love like love for family."

"Even though Joe was willing to kill somebody in the process? What makes him any different from any other criminal on the street?" he asked, showing absolutely no sign of breaking, talking to her as if Joe wasn't in the room.

"I know," she said. "I get that. And I get that, for you, this is a big deal."

"Yeah, it is a big deal," he said. "Just think if it was you or your father Joe was willing to kill."

She winced at that. "Right," she said. "It's easy to do something like this if it's not personal."

"Absolutely, but it *is* personal in this case," Eton said. "Very personal. This is my life we're talking about and the lives of my friends. We've all been to hell and back. So I want answers, and I want them now. Either you get answers for me or you step out of this room, and I'll get the answers my way."

She stood up tall and walked to Eton and damned if she stood toe-to-toe with him, glaring all the while. "This old man is hurt and not in very good shape emotionally, so you are not to threaten him."

He glared down at her, and she shook her head. "No, Eton," she said. "He's just an old man, trying to save his family."

"I know," he bit off. "But—" Then his voice trailed away, as he stared at her.

She shook her head. "No buts," she said gently. "This is what we have to deal with."

"If he doesn't talk, what do you suggest I do?"

Just then Joe started to talk.

She spun around, looked at Joe, and answered him in the same dialect. Finally, she turned to Eton and said, "He wants to talk. He is afraid that you're right and that they might come after him now."

"There's no *might* about it," Eton said. "He's a loose thread. Joe gave up his life the minute he got involved in this."

She looked at Eton and winced. "Do we have to say it quite so harshly?"

"The truth is the truth," he said.

She rejoined Joe at his bedside, sat down, and asked, "Who hired you to do this?"

"Karl," he said, "Karl Babinshe."

She frowned and said, "I know that name, but I don't know why."

"He's one of the old owners of a company here," Joe said. "He invested in that townhome property development the first time but not the second time."

"Why did he hire you, and what did he want you to do?"

Eton asked him.

"He said that we were to deliver you there and to leave. All he wanted was for us to take you there."

"And when did you know about this?"

"They contacted me after I saw you at the café," he said.

At that, Eton raised his gaze. "I knew I was being followed, but I didn't realize it was to that extent."

Joe nodded. "They follow you all the time," he said. He looked at Sammy and said, "You are in danger too."

"That's one of the reasons I'm here now," she said, "because I am in danger. Everybody is in danger. They've already killed your son, and you are next, and they tried to kill Eton."

"You should go away," Joe said abruptly to Sammy.

"What do you know about them?" Eton asked.

"I don't know anything," he said. "Karl asked me to do it as a favor. I told him that I didn't want to do anything illegal, and he said that it wasn't. That I would just take you up there. Then, when I got there, and I went inside the building to tell him that you were on the way, nobody was there. Instead, I was attacked from behind." He reached up to his head. "I'm too old for this shit," he muttered.

"Then you shouldn't have gotten into the game in the first place," Eton said. "How do I find this Karl guy?"

"He has a big home up around the next town," he said. "He spends a lot of time walking in the hills."

"Did he give you a reason why he wanted to see me?"

"He said that somebody else needed something from you, and he'd been asked to get it."

"That's very nebulous," Eton said.

Joe nodded. "I know. I'm sorry," he said. "I didn't want to do it. I knew I shouldn't have. I shouldn't have gotten

DALE MAYER

involved at all," he said. "It's not who I want to be."

"Or who your wife would like you to be," Sammy reminded him. At that, Joe looked out the window. "I almost wish I were dead now," he said, "and that I could be with her."

"Not yet," Eton said, "but, if you keep it up, it will be that way. Then you've left your grandson with nobody to help him."

"A lot of money was involved," Joe said. "More money than I could ever make."

"That's how they do it," Eton said. "They find your weakness, and they exploit it." That was something that Eton himself could really understand. He didn't like it, but he understood it. He looked down at Sammy, saw the soft look on her face, and sighed. He turned to Joe. "What else can you tell me?"

"I don't know," he said. "I just don't know."

"Do you have his contact information?"

"He phoned me," he said.

"And how is he to pay you?"

"The money arrived in my bank today," he said.

"I want the account number," Eton said. "So we can track it back."

"You don't think it came from him?"

"Oh, it probably did," he said, "but I need to figure out who gave it to him. I need the account that it came from."

"Oh," he said. He hesitated. "Will you take away the money?"

At that, Sammy leaned forward, patted his hand, and said, "Eton won't. But I don't know about the police."

At that, his face crestfallen, Joe nodded and said, "Right. I guess the police have to be called, don't they?"

"Well, you did accept money to help get me killed," Eton said, with a cool tone. He was prepared to give Joe somewhat of a pass, but Eton didn't want to let him off the hook completely.

At that, Joe just nodded and stared down at the bedsheet.

"What about your son Harry? What was he involved in?"

"He was hired by Karl to make a bunch of phone calls that they needed done."

"Up at the building complex?"

"Yeah, he'd come up when I was there," he said, "and use the phones up there. Where nobody knew what he was doing or where he was."

"So, tell me everything you can about the work you did for Karl," he ordered, "and everything you saw." By the time Joe was done talking, Eton understood that his son Harry was probably as much of a dupe as Joe was. "Has your son ever held down a regular job?"

"Yes, but not for long," Joe admitted. "He's always had big plans that never materialized. He's the baby who came into our lives later. We took him in as a baby, never could legally adopt him, so kept his name as is and treated him as our own," he said. "We spoiled him. I know we shouldn't have, but we did. Now he's gone."

Just then a knock came at the door, and a nurse stepped in. She quickly ushered them out. The last thing Eton said to Joe was, "I'll see what security we can set up for you. Besides that we'll see you tomorrow."

Joe nodded, and then the door closed.

As they walked out of the hospital, Sammy asked, "Now what?"

"Now I go visit this Karl guy," he said. "And now that I

have Joe's bank account number, I backtrack that payment." He'd already texted the number to Garret, who passed it on to other members of the team. "We should have answers soon." He led the way to the vehicle, and, as they got to the parking lot, the Spidey sense on the back of his neck started to tingle.

"Stay close," he said, his hand reaching to his back, where he kept his lower back holster. He turned and looked around again.

She snuggled up close and asked, "What is it?"

"We're being watched for one thing," he said, "but it might be worse than that."

He walked to the car, which was Joe's car, then walked around it ever-so-slowly.

"What's the matter?"

He gave her a sideways look. "Well, just a few hours ago, when I got into a vehicle, it blew up."

She winced and said, "Maybe we should go back inside and wait for alternative transportation."

"Not a bad idea," he said, and he quickly led her inside. He already had his phone out, arranging for a ride. When Garret called him back ten minutes later, he said, "Give it about two minutes, then walk out to the front, and I should be there."

He looked at her and said, "We're about to get our ride home."

"Good," she said nervously. "But how do we know if it's safe?"

"Because it's Garret," he said.

"How did he get here so fast?"

"He was already coming in behind us," he said. "We needed to make sure we had more backup than last time."

He didn't add that Garret had come without Eton's knowledge, but it made perfect sense that he would. Just as Eton was ready to step out, a large truck with leather and chrome drove up to the front of the hospital. "This is him," Eton said, and he rushed her out the door and into the front of the big truck, giving her a hand up. He jumped in right behind her, the whole thing happening in a matter of seconds. As soon as they were in, Garret hit the gas and pulled away.

"Will we just leave Joe's car?" Sammy asked.

"Yes, but we'll have Ice send a team to check it out and to make sure it's safe."

CHAPTER 11

WHEN SAMMY GOT back to her place, she didn't want to end up alone in the house. She hated to say goodbye. Looking at the two men, still seated in the truck, she asked, "Do you want to come in?"

They hesitated, and Garret said, "We can come in for a few minutes."

Eton looked at him and said, "Maybe you should head back."

"No way, we are staying together," he said.

"Any reason?" she asked lightly, as she hopped from the vehicle, but they rushed her inside right away. She looked up at Eton, as the door closed behind them. "Were we followed?"

"No, not that we saw," he said, "but that doesn't mean we didn't miss somebody."

"Right, in other words, I'm in danger."

"Anybody involved in this deal is in danger," he said. He looked around at the house and smiled. "An architect's dream."

"It was my parents' dream home," she said, with a faint smile. She headed to the stairs, as she realized just how late it was. "My father should be asleep," she said.

"Do me a favor," he said, walking around. "Go upstairs, and just check to make sure that he's there."

She shot him a startled look and raced to her father's bedroom. Thankfully she saw his head poking out from under the covers. As she came downstairs, she sank into an armchair. "Don't scare me like that," she said in a harsh whisper.

"It's a different story when it's personal, isn't it?" he said, with a sideways glance.

She nodded. "I know," she said. "I was trying to be easy on Joe because you weren't."

"There's a time and a place," he said, "but we needed answers."

She nodded. "Is my father in danger?"

"I can't say for sure because I don't know how deep or how long this thing goes." He looked at Garret, as he sat down, even now already on his laptop. "Any updates?" Eton asked Garret.

"Some. We have a history on this Karl guy. We have his bank account, and now we've seen where the transfer to Joe came from. It was his account, but there is money in and out of that account on a steady basis that we are tracking down even now," he said.

Eton looked at her and asked, "Any chance of coffee?"

"Certainly," she said and hopped up. As she went into the kitchen, Eton sat down beside Garret. "What aren't you telling me?"

She could still hear them from the kitchen and deliberately listened in.

"One, the door was tampered with when we got here."

Eton nodded. "I saw that."

"So you can't leave her alone," Garret said.

"I wasn't planning on it. Next?"

"Ice says that Karl has connections to a big security

company in Africa."

He looked at him in shock. "What connections?"

"He has funded some small jobs around the world, and he fancies himself a bit of an arms dealer."

"Well, that's not good news. What company in Africa?"

"Apparently our main competitor," he said.

Eton sat here and stared at him. "Are you talking about Kingdom Securities?"

"Yep," Garret said. "We've never had any problems with them before though."

"I don't believe it," Eton said. "We've even done jobs with them."

"I know. Obviously this Karl guy has also funded a few jobs through them."

"That doesn't make any sense," Eton murmured.

"So far, none of it does, but we are finding more and more players every day, so potentially this may be the origin of the whole thing. Do you think it's the boss, or do you think somebody else in that company—like Krager—may want to stage a takeover or create a splinter group or what?"

"In this case it could be somebody in the company," Eton surmised.

"We've known that Krager sometimes has a hard time keeping control of his hires."

"That's what I was wondering," Eton said, "and I suppose it's possible that, by trying to take out our team, Krager would increase business for himself."

"Only if he was planning to take over Kingdom," Garret said. "And, if that's the case, there's no ceiling to the trouble they could create." Garret stared at Eton for a moment. "Are you willing to go back to the chalet, or should we both stay with her here?" Garret asked, shrugging.

"It's probably not fair to her father to have both of us moving in here," he said, with half a smile.

"No, probably not, but then maybe we should take her and move her up with us."

"And that won't happen either," Eton said, shaking his head.

"No, she won't leave her father. Particularly after you asked her to check on him," Garret said.

He reached up, rubbed his face. "I was trying to keep her out of any danger."

"Sometimes danger comes to us, and we don't have any choice. You know that."

"I know, but I don't like it."

"Of course not, especially since you've found someone you care for," he said, "and now you don't want to see that destroyed."

At that, Eton shot him a hard look.

"Hey, I'm just calling it as it is," he said.

"Yet you were part of the push to see her again."

"Absolutely, and I am not at all upset that this is where you are heading," he said. "We just have to find a way to keep her safe."

Eton had to admit, of all the things his partner had said, *that* made the most sense, and it showed the kind of man Garret was. He wasn't complaining about the extra complication; he wasn't saying Eton should walk away and leave her. Garret was all about joining forces to keep her safe. And that Eton appreciated very much.

Sammy heard part of their discussion from the kitchen, and it bothered her to think that level of danger was around them. That they thought her father might be in danger as well broke her heart. That was the last thing she needed for him. What was the answer though? Somehow Joe had gotten her embroiled in something that she didn't think he expected. And knowing the man as she did, she couldn't believe he had any ill intent and wanted to bring it down on her shoulders. She'd known him since she was little.

But she also knew what it was like to try to save those who you loved. And she had no doubts that Joe loved his family. That son of his had been a bit of a rascal, for sure. But it all was what it was, and the reality was that, if it hadn't been Joe, eventually it probably would have been someone else. That left her and her father, plus Eton and Garret, where they were now, left to figure out what they were supposed to do about it.

That's where the challenge came in. Trying to find an answer to all this. Answers that had apparently proven elusive so far. When the coffee was ready, she walked into the other room. "Well, if you two are done discussing what to do about me," she said, "do you take anything in your coffee?"

Her delivery was so smooth that it took both men a moment to understand what she had said.

Garret's face broke into a bright grin. "I like you," he said. "Good attitude."

She stared at him. "Not really a whole lot of choice in the matter, is there?"

"No, none at all," he said. "So let's be sensible about it from the beginning."

"Do you have any idea what we can do?" she asked Eton curiously, as she poured the coffee.

"Well, the one thing is to keep you and your father safe because not keeping you safe isn't an option."

"Says you," she said. "But that doesn't mean it'll be easy to do."

"No, of course not, but it's not impossible either."

"I wonder," she murmured, "and you're still not answering me."

"One of us will stay with you at all times," Garret said.

She looked up in shock. "That can't happen," she said. "You need to back him up." Pointing to Eton, she continued. "This one keeps getting into trouble."

At that, Garret burst out laughing. "Isn't that the truth?" he said affectionately.

She fisted her hands on her hips and glared at him. "You think I'm joking?"

"Doesn't matter if you're joking or not," he said, "because Eton is a born protector. He will not let anything happen to you and will keep you safe, regardless."

"Sure, but I don't want him looking after me if he is supposed to be out there finding the guy who's going after all of you."

"Exactly," Garret said. "At the same time, we now have a name, *Karl*. And we're tracing to find the person who paid him, and he has connections we are especially interested in, so we need to pay Karl a visit."

"Uh-huh."

Just then a vehicle came up the road, lights flashing around the room as it drove past. But it slowed down at the driveway. She frowned, as she saw the lights drift closer. "Most people don't slow down when they get here." Just then she heard an odd popping sound. She stared at the two men, but Garret had already raced to the window, and Eton had grabbed her and tossed her to the floor. Glass shattered seconds before she went down, as the window in front of them broke.

The moment it broke, something on fire landed on the

rug and the wood floor underneath, immediately hunting eagerly for its next source of fuel. She wanted to scream but she was too shocked, as she slowly picked herself up. The men were immediately on the Molotov cocktail, or whatever the thing was called, and were trying to put out the fire. She bolted to her feet, raced to the kitchen, and grabbed water, as the flames were even now licking at the curtains at the sides of the window. She tossed water on them, quickly dousing the flames.

As she went back to get more, she turned around to see the men had picked up the area rug and tossed it on top of the couch that was burning now too. She stared at them in shock. "Is this what trouble you meant?" she asked faintly.

"Well, I was hoping it's not what I meant," Garret said grimly. "But now it's definitely not safe for you here."

"You don't understand," she said blankly. "I can't leave my father here, and he won't leave."

"If you say so," he said. "What happens when he finds out about this?"

"I don't know," she whispered, not even sure how to explain it to him. "He won't do what I want him to do most of the time."

"What is his situation? How much longer does he have?" Eton asked. His question was direct but gentle.

She sighed, then closed her eyes for a moment and said, "He may well have run out of time," she said. "He's lived beyond the estimate the doctor gave him."

"Didn't you say something about seeking more treatment?"

"He seemed to rally a bit yesterday, or maybe it was today," she said, with a shrug. "I'm losing track of the days. But he said that maybe he should go find out if there is any other treatment. Like, get a second opinion."

"What's wrong with him exactly?"

"Stage four cancer," she said, "but it's not following the path the doctors expected. He's got a brain tumor as well, which compounds the problem."

"Wow, either one of those would kill him."

"He sleeps most of the time, though he finished the job we needed to get finished today," she said, with half a smile. "It's the last of his commitments."

"What are the chances that he just wanted to finish that before going to bed?"

"Well, he was truly excited about the idea of me having a date," she said drily. "He said that he wanted to see me settled, first and foremost."

"*Settled* is an old-fashioned term, isn't it?"

"He's an old-fashioned man," she said, with a gentle smile. "What do we do about this now?" she asked.

Even as she stood here, Garret had slipped out of the room and returned with a broom and was busy cleaning up the floor. He looked at her and asked, "Do you have a vacuum?"

She nodded. One of the rugs was badly burned on the side. "I suppose that should just go outside," she said.

"It would help with the smoke smell, yes," Garret said, "and I suggest you remove these two curtain panels that burned, maybe move that one over. How often do you close this?"

"Almost never."

"In that case, nobody would notice." Quickly he lifted the curtain rod from the wall and dropped off the two panels, hooks and all. He slid the other good panel down, so now instead of two panels at each end, there was one each.

Then he hung it back up. "Once we get this cleaned up and take this rug out," he said, "it's just the window."

She stood here, stunned. "Wow, you've minimized that damage pretty fast," she said, and, even as she spoke, he was removing the rug. She sighed. "I suppose the insurance might cover this."

"It's hard to say. I don't know what your policies are like over here," Eton said. "A big window like that will be expensive, even though the damage is just on the one side." Then he shrugged and said, "Honestly the whole thing would have to come out."

"I'm sure it will," she said. She turned and looked at the both of them and said, "Neither of you went after him. Why?"

"Because he was already being tracked," Eton said quietly.

She stopped and stared at him. "What?"

He gave her a half smile. "We're not alone," he said.

She stopped and stared. "Are you saying what I think you are saying? That more of you are out here?"

"Well, we definitely have eyes in the sky," Garret said. "I'll check in with them in about a minute."

As he straightened the curtains on the rod, she just couldn't believe it. "I guess it makes sense that more people are out there with you," she said, "but I'm not sure whether I understand what the 'eye in the sky' comment means."

"We are part of a big team. Remember?" Eton said. "I told you that the entire team has been targeted."

She nodded slowly. "Right. It just seems like so much craziness has happened these last few days," she said. "I'm not sure what I remember and what seems like so long ago now that I just found out this morning." She shook her head.

"Yes, sometimes it happens that way," Garret said. "And Eton just checked in with our team. They're on it."

"Good," she said. "I'm glad."

"You and me both," Garret said.

"So does that mean it's safe to leave me alone now?" she asked hopefully. Although she didn't have a clue how that was supposed to work because, if she were safe to be alone, why had she just been targeted?

"It's hard to say," Eton said, "but we won't take a chance anyway."

She took a deep breath. "I get that," she said. "I'm just not so sure what any of this means."

"It means that we don't take any chances," he said. "It's all about safety."

"Right," she said, frowning. "I think I'd like that coffee now."

"Me too," Garret said.

Just then Eton's cell buzzed. He took one look, glanced at Garret, and said, "I'm gone."

Garret nodded, and, just like that, Eton bolted out the door.

She turned and looked at Garret, then spun around as she heard the big truck whip by, probably to follow the vehicle that had thrown the firebomb. "Did he just take off like that, after you guys decided I shouldn't be left alone?"

"You aren't alone," he said. "I'm not exactly an invalid." Enough indignation was in his voice that she turned and apologized immediately.

"I'm sorry, Garret," she said. "I didn't mean it like that."

"Yes, you did," he said, with a sniff.

She had to smile. "Okay, but I just was thinking that he

would stay with me."

"Of course you were because you want him to."

"Well, maybe," she said, "I'm not so sure about that though."

"It's all good," he said, chuckling. "I'm just tripping you up to get you to admit that you wanted him here."

She shot him a look.

He smirked, as he shook his head. "You can get a lot of information across with that look in your eyes," he said, smiling broadly.

"Well, it's definitely interesting to be around you guys," she said. "I didn't realize how damn boring my life was before I met you two."

"Hey, we are good people," he said.

"I know," she replied. "I really wanted him to behave himself at the hospital with Joe, and the only reason he did, I'm sure, is because he knew how much it mattered to me."

"If he was doing anything other than beating the crap out of Joe, you have an amazing influence over him," he said seriously. "Think about what Joe did to him. To all of us. It's a miracle that Eton wasn't killed by that car bomb."

"I know," she whispered. "And I'm just now realizing it, as I see my own father's life in danger."

"Exactly," he said. "And for what? Money?"

"In Joe's case, money translates to his grandson's health," she said, "so it's understandable."

"Understandable, but he sacrificed a lot of other people for that, including his own son."

"Except he had no idea it would end that way."

"That's the trouble with guys like this," Garret said quietly. "It *always* ends that way."

She winced and nodded. "Hopefully you guys can bring

this to a fast conclusion, so there is no more trouble."

"We'd like to think so, but, so far, nothing is going very fast."

She sank into the couch beside him, studying the room. "I don't know if my father will notice," she whispered. Except that one side of the couch was torched and damaged.

He looked at it and asked, "Do you have a blanket, like a throw or something, to put over that?"

"Yes, but it still smells in here."

"It does, but the fresh air coming through the window will help clean it up. We'll get wood hauled in to nail up here, while you await a window replacement."

She muttered slowly, "Everything has gone so crazy these last couple days."

"Your friend is gone too, isn't she?"

"Yes, and I don't even understand how that happened so fast," she says. "It's like she suddenly realized she was in danger, and that was it. She was gone."

"Do you blame her?"

"No, of course not," she said, "and she is a really good friend, so obviously I want to keep her safe."

"Exactly, and now, with her gone, hopefully she is safe."

"I hope so," she whispered. "This is all just too confusing."

"Not really," he said. "When you think about it, it's really simple."

"Is it?"

"Yes," he said. "It is. All we have to do is keep you and your father safe."

"Plus keeping you and Eton safe." She gave a broken laugh. "I'm not so sure that's such an easy thing to do either," she whispered.

He smiled and said, "Some things in life are just the way they are, so we'll do our best."

She nodded slowly. "I get that. I really do," she said. "It's just a very confusing state of affairs for me."

"Yeah, it is, especially when seen from an outsider's point of view. However, for us, who have more experience with this crap, it's not impossible," he said.

She took a slow deep breath. "I can get through this. If you guys can, I can."

He laughed. "It's not a contest," he said gently. "A lot of things in life we would just as soon not have to deal with."

"I think that goes for all of us," she said, with a nod toward her father's bedroom.

"Exactly." Garret nodded in understanding. "Why don't you go to bed and rest?" he suggested.

She stared at him in shock. "Are you serious? It's not like I'll leave and go to sleep."

"Well, I had hoped you might try," he said. "I just thought maybe you could."

"Not happening," she said, with a smile. "Not until I know Eton is safe."

"See? I knew you cared," he said, with a knowing nod.

She rolled her eyes at him. "Yes, but I shouldn't. I don't know anything about him. I don't know anything about either of you guys, and honestly, it's all happening just way too fast."

"Nothing is way too fast yet," he said, "because nothing has happened yet. You're just interested. Okay, maybe a little more than that," he said, smiling at the look she'd shot at him.

She smiled back, nodded, and said, "True enough."

"So don't get scared," he said.

"You want me to have a relationship with him, don't you?"

"Yes, but only with the caveat that it's right for both of you. I would be happy to see him with somebody special in his life. He's spent so much of his life doing good for others in the worst of conditions, yet rarely has anybody been there for him. He has the team, of course, but nobody special, just for him, you know?"

"I do, and that's hard," she said, "and I know exactly how it feels."

"Of course you do," he said. "That's one of the reasons you are perfect for him. Because you do understand."

"Maybe," she said, "but I won't be pushed into anything."

He chuckled at that. "So far it appears that you're the one doing the pushing."

She stopped, stared at him, and realized that, in a way, he was right.

ETON PICKED UP the pace, driving as fast as he could in the dark with the headlights off, as he tracked the vehicle that was a good ten minutes ahead of him. His phone beside him was connected to Ice.

"I'm handing you over to Stone right now," Ice said. "He's got the truck on satellite."

"Tell me where I'm going," he said to Stone. "Make it good."

"Okay," he said, "we've got him. He's slowing down and taking a left-hand turn, which appears to be down some dark road around to another village."

"I believe it. This whole area is dotted with small

towns."

"Well, he's heading up to another property."

"I'm pushing hard behind him, so keep giving me instructions."

"Pull off and sit on the side of the road," Stone said.

Immediately Eton pulled onto the shoulder and asked, "Why? What's up?"

"Because you'll catch up to him too fast," he said. "Just sit there for a minute, while I wait and see what he'll do." As he waited, Eton heard Stone give a sigh of satisfaction. "Okay, looks like he's parked."

"Interesting," Eton said.

"Yes, it looks like it may be home base for him."

"Sweet, that would be perfect," he said. "I want to go in and beat the shit out of somebody. They tried to torch Sammy's house."

"I heard about that," Stone said. "The world never changes, does it?"

"Nope, assholes are everywhere," he said. "So can I go now?"

"Yes, go slow, stick to the right-hand side, and a pretty steep section is coming up," he said. "I want you to park at the bottom of that and then turn the vehicle around, so you've got your getaway vehicle on a bit of the shoulder off to the side."

"I can do that," he said, and he followed the instructions exactly because the one thing about having eyes in the sky was that they had access to information that he did not. As soon as he found the steep section, he immediately turned around, pulled into a small shoulder area and pulled off onto the far side and blended the dark truck into the trees. Then he got out and slipped through the trees, his phone still at his side, as he climbed up the steep section of the hill. "Where am I going?"

"On the left is a garage. I thought I saw a door open," he said, "but I can't be too sure if it's open or closed now. The shadows are weird."

"Okay, I'm almost there. Thanks. I'm signing out."

"Good luck," Stone said.

Eton raced up to the side of the house and flattened himself against the back of the house and waited. Absolutely nothing else was here. He remained against the building and waited until his heart stilled and his mind focused. The garage was open. "Good," he murmured. He slipped inside the first corner and waited in the darkness, until his eyes adjusted. A door was up ahead that he had seen from the outside on his way in. This garage was attached to a huge house. He was hoping it was the guy's home but no way to know at this point. Eton also didn't know if any security was here, whether personnel or hardware. He quickly sent a message to Stone, asking him if he had any way to check. Stone responded, saying he was on it.

And, with that, Eton pocketed his phone, made his way over, and hid himself against the door connecting the garage to the house. The garage itself was massive, big enough to hold four vehicles. But only one was here, and that was the truck he'd followed. It gleamed black and chrome, very high-end all the way, slightly dusty, but that made sense, given the location where this guy lived.

Eton tested the doorknob, and the knob turned easily under his hand. He pushed the door open ever-so-slightly and stepped inside. Nothing but silence. He tilted his head, trying to figure out who was where and how many were inside. No way to do a heat scan inside the building from the satellite at this distance, especially with all the tree cover. They could catch figures outside but not inside, which was too damn bad because Eton was going in blind here, and he had no physical onsite backup. His only backup at this point was Garret and Stone, via technology. And Stone just confirmed these very thoughts.

As Eton moved forward, he checked out the room closest to him, a laundry room. He kept on going through, deeper into the house, until he came upon the living room. There he stopped and studied the area, but it was empty, no sign of anyone. The dining room was empty, and, as he got to the kitchen, he noted an open bottle of scotch on the counter and a glass with about two inches in it. But, of the drinker, no sign. That made Eton suspicious as hell. He immediately withdrew, until he heard a toilet flush and a door open. As he watched, his prey came out, snatched up the glass and tossed back the liquor. Eton quickly and silently walked around, so he'd come up to him in a better position. As Eton stepped forward, he took his handgun and pressed it against the man's ear. "You're the one I want to talk to," he said.

The man froze.

"Put down the scotch," Eton said and slowly the man lowered the drink. And then, with the gun still pressed against him, Eton led him over to the kitchen chair, where he sat him down hard and knocked him out with one punch. He had to work fast now and yanked his hands behind his back. Pulling handcuffs from his pocket, Eton quickly clipped his hands together. Then, knowing it wouldn't be hard for his prisoner to stand up and to loop his arms around his feet and back to the front of him, Eton searched through the kitchen and found some zip ties and quickly bound his hands to the chair and then his feet too, both supertight. With the man now securely tied, he was slowly coming to.

Eton smiled. "Are you alone?"

The man just glared at him.

"In that case, I'll go check it out myself," he said, "and see if I need to take care of anybody else."

He quickly searched the house, but it was empty. With a quick text to Stone, giving him Eton's status, Eton headed back to the dining room. He smiled as he shifted the man's clothing so he could pull out his wallet. And, sure enough, it was Karl. "Hi, Karl," he said. "Do you know me?"

The man shook his head.

"Well, you should," he said. "You wanted me brought up to the townhome lot." At that, the man's eyes widened. "Yeah, I lived through the explosion. Didn't you know that?" he said. "Of course Joe is badly hurt. He's in the hospital, and his son's dead, compliments of you. But then you thought that you should try to burn down Sammy's house," he said. "How the hell does that work?"

The man just shook his head. "I didn't have anything to do with that."

"And you are lying," he said.

"I am not," he said. "I didn't have anything to do with that."

"Well, I saw you throw that Molotov cocktail into the house," he said. "I was in there too, but, by the time we got the fires put out and everything cleaned up, I decided to let you get home, so you could feel safe for a little bit," he said, with half a smile. "But I'm here now, so let's have a talk."

"I don't know anything about this," he said. "You're just bluffing."

"No, not true. You were tracked by satellite, by the way,

so you can give up the lies."

His eyes widened at the idea of satellite surveillance.

Most people don't think there are eyes in the sky, even when they consider the type of jobs they were involved in.

"That can't be," he said quietly.

"Did you really think Kingdom Securities wouldn't keep track of what you were doing?"

At that, the other man paled in fright.

"Oh, yeah," Eton said. "Just because you're dealing with one of them doesn't mean somebody else doesn't know what's going on," he said, with a knowing smile.

"That can't be," he said. "I don't have anything to do with them."

"Well, that's bullshit," he said. "You see? We've already checked your bank accounts. We already checked the amount of money you paid Joe to deliver me." Eton paused. "I'm insulted by the small figure, by the way. I'm worth more than that, you know?" he said, sneering.

But the man now shook his head rapidly. "Look. I do business with them, that's all."

"That's all that was to you, right? Just business?"

He swallowed hard. "You don't understand."

"You're right. I don't," he said. "This is all bullshit, as far as I'm concerned. My friends have been attacked. You've tried to kill several of us, and now you're after Sammy. And what you did to Joe, preying on his need to save his grandson like that? It's a damn shame."

The man just kept shaking his head. "You don't understand. You don't understand."

"No, I don't," he said. "So you better tell me, so I do understand." He waited for Karl to speak. "Your chance to do that is running out. So start talking now."

The man stared at him, as if trying to figure out what to say.

"Only the truth and do it now. I don't have time for any more bullshit," he said.

"You don't know what these people are like."

"Buddy, you don't know what I'm like," he said in a hard voice. "So start talking."

He just shook his head.

Eton lifted a hand and backhanded him in a swift move. "You really think I'm here to play games?" he asked.

"They will kill me," he said.

"Don't you realize you're already dead?" he said, with a feral smile. "Because, once they know that I'm here, you're history. They already know, by the way. It's just that simple. You were history the minute you got involved with them."

He kept shaking his head, as if trying not to believe it, yet something was in his gaze that said he already had a good idea. "It can't be," he said. "It wasn't supposed to be like this."

"Of course not. It's never supposed to be like this," he said. "But guess what? It almost always ends up this way."

"No," he said, "that's not fair."

"*Fair?*" Eton said. "Now that's a really interesting comment. What is fair about playing Joe? His son is dead. You torched Sammy's place. What is fair about that?"

Karl just stared at him and said, "I wasn't supposed to get found out. I didn't want to do this. I didn't want to work on Joe at all. He knows me."

"So why did you?" Eton asked curiously.

"Because somebody I know said I had to. Plus they had something on me."

"That seems to be the way of the world, doesn't it, Karl?

You do something, and nobody lets you forget it."

"And I didn't even do anything wrong," he said bitterly. "But I didn't want to open it up to the world either."

"And that weakness is what got you in trouble," he said.

"Yes, and now you're here," Karl said.

"Apparently these guys really like exploiting the weaknesses in people," Eton said.

"That's not all they do," he said. "You know that, as soon as we're caught, we're dead anyway."

"That's exactly what I just said to you," he said.

"I'm not here alone either," Karl said. "I was hoping they'd come and rescue me, but now I suspect they'll just be here to take us both out."

"Does that explain the whiskey?"

"I was asked on my way in if I'd stopped to make sure the job was done, and of course I hadn't, so they were not impressed," he said. "I wondered then if I'd crossed a line."

"It's a good thing you didn't check because it would have meant that the fire would have been much worse, but instead we put it out fairly quickly. They would know that too by now."

He nodded calmly. "I didn't want to hurt Joe, and they didn't like that either."

"What they don't like," Eton said, "is resistance."

"Arguing over Joe got me into trouble."

"Well, don't look to me for sympathy," he said, searching the area, "and you can help yourself by helping me."

"Why would I do that?" Karl asked. "I've already been paid a ton of money."

"Well, you can't access it," he said. "We've frozen your accounts."

Karl stared at him in shock. "You can't do that," he said.

"Watch me," Eton replied.

Just then rapid gunfire came through the living room window. Eton hit the floor and bolted backward behind the kitchen island, even as he watched another spray coming through, crossing the living room and hitting Karl right in the head. Swearing, Eton raced through the kitchen's rear patio doors and outside. The worse thing he could do was get caught up inside like that.

Once he was outside, he checked the surroundings and bolted for the trees. It was already way too late for Karl, so what Eton had to do was make sure he was safe, and then all he could think about was Garret and Sammy. He bolted through the trees, back down to the base of the house, and yet, as he went past, he saw another vehicle firing multiple gunshots into the house, followed by something that looked like a grenade.

When, all of a sudden, he heard an explosion, he realized it was a small bomb, and the house just went up in smoke. He stared at the house, realizing how much destruction these guys were hell-bent on doing, with no consideration for those inside. As he analyzed the situation, the vehicles took off in front of him. He raced down to his truck, hoping they hadn't seen it. When they bolted past it at top speed, he hopped in and headed out after them.

All he could think about at that point in time was that they were heading toward Sammy's house. He quickly called Garret and screamed into his phone as soon as Garret answered. "They shot Karl and completely torched his house with military-grade explosives," he said. "Get the hell out of there right now. They are heading back, and I don't know if they're coming for you or not."

"We're on it," Garret said.

"Just keep yourselves safe. I'm behind the assholes," he said. "I don't give a shit if they see me at this point. I want to make sure I chase them away from you guys."

"How far out are you?"

"Twelve minutes," he said, "probably the longest of my life." After a pause, he said, "Stay safe, brother." Then he threw down the phone, slammed his foot harder onto the gas, and roared forward. If they torched Sammy's place the same way they just did Karl's, it wouldn't matter if they were inside or not. Anything even nearby would go up regardless. All he could do was hope they got her father out safely. Because this plan had just gone all to shit.

CHAPTER 12

SAMMY LEANED AGAINST the busted living room window, staring out into the night. An explosion had occurred somewhere only moments ago. Garret started moving, the phone to his ear. Shoving it back in his pocket, he snatched up his laptop and said sternly, "Get your father, fast. We've got trouble coming even faster. We have to get away from the house."

She stared at him in shock and bolted toward her father's room. "Dad, Dad, wake up!" she called.

No answer. When he slept, he slept so damn hard these days. She heard Garret rushing around, presumably picking up whatever equipment he needed. She raced over to her father's side and gave him a good shake. Hard enough that he should wake up. His head moved a little to the side but no reaction other than that.

She stared at him in shock, and, reaching down, she hesitantly placed two fingers against his neck, looking for a pulse. There wasn't one. She placed a hand on his chest and then her ear, searching for any signs of life. But, when she lifted his hand and dropped it, it fell, completely lifeless. She turned to the doorway, where Garret stared at her. "He's gone," she whispered. "I think he's gone."

Garret, his expression somber, raced over and checked for himself. He nodded and said, "Come on. Let's go."

"We can't just leave him here," she cried out, but Garret ushered her from the bedroom.

He asked, "What about your work?"

She looked at him, shrugged, and said, "It's all in the cloud."

"Passport, purse?"

She stared at him in shock but snatched her passport and put it in her purse, grabbed a sweater, and put on shoes.

"Let's go. Move, move, move," he said, pushing her out the back door of the kitchen.

"What the hell is going on?" she cried out. Her heart was still in the house with her father. She couldn't believe that he had died just like that, while she was in the living room. It just seemed so wrong.

At the same time, it seemed so very right. Of all the most peaceful ways to go, in his sleep had to be it. But why? Why right now? He had seemed to be holding his own. Certainly he'd been declining, but she had no indication that today was the day. She didn't have a chance to even think about it because Garret was now pushing her to the hillside behind the house.

"Climb," he said, "fast."

His demeanor didn't leave room for anything but complete and absolute compliance. She didn't know what the hell was going on, but it was obviously serious. She heard vehicles rushing down the road and realized he was trying to get her well out of the way from whatever those guys would do. With that realization, fear lent wings to her feet, and she raced up the hill, carrying just her purse. She thought of all the things in the house they could destroy but hoped that none of it would come to pass. He'd wanted her to grab necessities, which in her world was just her purse because it had her wallet and credit cards. But then she thought of all the mementos of her life in there. Still, she had had no time, and he kept pushing her.

"Up, up, up," he said.

Finally she reached the top of the hillside and collapsed to the ground, raggedly gasping for breath. "What the hell?" she asked.

He said, "Look."

She turned back to see her house burning bright. "Oh, God," she cried out. "No, no!" She stood and tried to race down the hill, but he wouldn't let her. He grabbed her, threw her to the ground, and held her there.

"You can't go," he said.

She stared at him, her eyes brimming with tears. "My father," she said.

"He was already gone. If we had tried to move him, we'd have become fuel for the fire. Just ask yourself how your father would feel about leaving this earth—body and soul—along with one of his greatest creations, surrounded by all of his memories," he said.

She just stared at him. "Surely we can stop it."

"I'm sure the fire engines are already on the way," he whispered. "What we can't know is whether the guys who did this have left or if they're lurking somewhere to see if they succeeded."

She shook her head. "It's just too much."

He held her close, and they both heard the buzzing of his phone. He pulled it out and said, "It's Eton." She snatched the phone from his hands. "Eton, we're up the mountain behind the house," she said, "my house."

"I know," he said. "I'm so sorry."

"How could they do this?" she wailed.

"I'll be there in a few minutes," he said.

"No," she said, her voice a bit stronger. "You catch those assholes."

He hesitated.

"Listen. I know your people are probably tracking them. Don't waste time coming up here. We're fine. Just go after them and learn what you can."

With that, he hung up.

She stared down at her home, feeling tears in the corner of her eyes. She realized she was also looking at her father's funeral pyre. "I just—" And she stopped.

"Sometimes," Garret said, "life just happens. The good thing is that your father had already passed in his sleep. All things considered, that's the very best outcome we could have had here."

She stopped, thought about it, and slowly nodded. "As much as I don't want to think that way, you're right," she said. "It's just so sad, though and quite a shock."

"The sad part," he said, "is that your father passed away. The house is just a house. And you're an architect. You can rebuild it wherever. Your father was already gone, so his death was not a part of this fire. Honestly, it's pretty hard to argue with the fact that he died in his sleep. That's an awesome way to go. But, like any death, it's still a shock and leaves behind those who mourn the loss."

"And that is something I won't get used to very quickly," she muttered.

"And you don't have to," he said gently. "What you need is time to grieve, time to deal with the loss."

"I haven't even dealt with the fact that we just found him like that, much less the house," she said. "My mind just keeps running through everything that was in there."

"The only thing that was in there of value," he said, "you'd already lost."

She sniffled back tears, as she nodded slowly. "I know," she said, "but—" And she just waved her hand at the fire burning strong and bright below.

"I know," he said. "It's a lot of loss all at once. But it is something you can handle."

"Maybe," she said. "I'm just not in very good shape right now."

"Of course not," he said. "Nobody's expecting you to be. You're in shock."

"Can you find those guys?" she asked, her voice getting stronger. "Can you help Eton?"

He looked at her hesitantly.

"Do what you can to help him," she said. "I'll just sit here and mourn."

"I can't have you racing back down there," he said, and she realized how much she was holding them back because he couldn't trust her.

"I promise," she said. "Nothing is there for me now."

"No," he said, "there isn't. But you'll have a new life after this."

She just didn't see how. As she settled into her own space, resting her back against a tree, she tried to calm down. Garret pulled out his laptop and his phone. She listened with half an ear as he contacted various people. She didn't know what was happening, but it sounded like something was, and, for that, she was grateful. She was thankful that people were out there they could call on right now because, damn it, she wanted these guys caught, and she wanted them to suffer for what they had done.

And, as Garret had said, she also needed to focus on the

fact that, although she'd lost her father, it hadn't been a result of the fire or the whole related scenario, and he didn't know anything about it. He went quietly in his sleep, and she could hardly argue with one of the most peaceful deaths she'd ever heard about. Now all she had to do was keep herself together, so she didn't impede their progress. She turned to look at Garret. "Let me know if there's anything I can do," she said in a firm voice.

He nodded, but he was distracted.

She stared down at the remnants of her house, wondering if she could possibly have identified any of the people involved. She wondered just who would have done this to her, yet suspected it was all based on this Karl, that Joe had told them about. "I would have thought dealing with Karl would be the end of it," she said.

"We didn't," he said, "but we were hoping it was a step up."

"So do you think this was hired out as well?"

"Definitely," he said, "Karl was also shot to clean up the loose ends."

"Oh, my God. If they've done that, then what about Joe?"

"We do have a guard on him, but I can't guarantee that his life is any more secure." He pulled out his phone and called the hospital. She listened, chewing on her bottom lip. When he turned, and she caught the odd look in his eyes, she cried out in pain. He said, "Thank you," into the phone and hung up. "Joe had a heart attack and didn't make it. We might never know if it was natural or from something else."

Her heart sank. "As far as I'm concerned, they killed him regardless. Why are they so worried about getting caught?"

"Because we won't stop," Garret said. "We won't stop

until we get these assholes." Just then he hopped to his feet and said, "I want you to stay here, Sammy. Don't move."

"Where are you going?" she asked.

"I'm switching places with Eton. The suspects disappeared in two separate directions. We're tracking one on satellite, and the other one is coming around to the village on the inside of this hill," he said, and he pointed down below where she saw lights. "I'll take it from here, and Eton's coming back to look after you."

"That doesn't make any sense."

He didn't bother explaining, and she realized he wasn't telling her a whole lot. But then he was gone. Just like that, he disappeared into the tree canopy, leaving her sitting here all alone.

ETON PULLED OFF to the side and drove up the hill partway. There he saw Garret, waiting for him, and he hopped out and asked, "Why the switch?"

"She needs you," Garret said.

Eton looked at him, startled. "Why? What's the matter?"

Garret quickly explained about her father and then said, "Satellites are tracking the other one. I'll follow this guy."

"Don't you get into any shit," he warned.

Garret laughed. "All we're doing is tracking down the bad guy, same as always. I'm also not too sure that hill is empty."

With that, Eton gave him a startled look and bolted to the top of the hill. By the time he got there, he'd been more concerned about speed than silence. When he reached the top, he stopped and frowned. No sign of Sammy at all. He slowly shifted through the trees, his movements silent as possible. But no sign of her. He pulled out his phone. And as soon as he did, a voice called out, "Garret?"

He froze and slowly lifted his head. "Who is there?" he said in a low voice, checking his back holster, silently cursing to find his gun missing. The last time he knew he had it was in Karl's house.

"Well, I've got something you want, and you've got something I want."

"And what is it that you want?" Eton said.

"I want you dead," he said, "and I'm quite happy to have it happen any way you want."

"Well, that won't happen," he said. "I've already decided I'll die from old age."

"I don't think so," he said. "The one thing I do know is you've been trying to protect this girl here. And I've got her."

"Why?" he asked in that conversational tone. "You took everything else away from her."

"She was supposed to be gone," he said. "That's not the point. It's you I want."

"What about Eton?"

"Oh, we'll take him out too. Don't you worry. We got vehicles following him all over the place."

"Says you," he said, leaning back, because there hadn't been anybody behind him when he was in that truck.

"Besides, he's only got so many lives. He escaped once, so he won't escape the second time."

With his blood running cold, he slipped through the trees to get a little closer to where the voice was coming from.

"I wouldn't take any more steps in that direction," the stranger said.

"Why is that?"

"Because I've got a gun against her head." With that, the man stepped out into the clearing. And, sure enough, Sammy was there, but, instead of crying and looking victimized, he saw fury building inside her. He could only hope that she held it back. He also hoped that she recognized his voice. He stayed hidden. "What now?"

"I want you to come forward," he said, "and then I'll shoot you nice and simple. That'll make it easy."

"You could still tell me why," he said. "I don't even know who the hell you are."

"I was Karl's boss," he said, "and we don't like the fact that you seem to think you're finding your way through this maze."

"What's the matter? Obviously you don't want to share your fees with anyone else. And you don't want to fight for future jobs. Come on. Just between you and me."

"Apparently not," he said, "and that sucks because we didn't intend on you even getting this close."

"Well, that's just too bad for you," he said. "We can take you out anytime."

"Well, I think that's what the bosses are a little worried about," he said.

"And why is that such an issue?" Eton asked.

"Because they have no intention of being found."

"Are you part of Kingdom Securities?"

"Wow," he said. "How the hell do you even know about them?" An odd tone was in his voice.

"What the hell are you talking about?" Eton asked. "Why wouldn't I know about them? Kingdom Securities is one of Bullard's competitors."

"Now Bullard—such an idiot," he said. "He's nowhere near as good as our guys are."

"So you're saying that you guys at Kingdom are trying to take us out, huh?"

"I didn't say that," he protested.

"No, maybe not, but you sure as hell aren't saying anything different," he said.

"I don't even know what it's all about."

"Why is somebody trying to take out Bullard?"

"What? Somebody did take out Bullard," he said, "no *trying to* about it."

"Has the kill been confirmed?" Eton asked curiously.

"So you don't know yet," he said. "That's pretty funny."

"It doesn't matter if it's funny or not," he said. "Answer the question."

"No, no confirmed killing yet. Are you telling me that he's still alive?"

Eton wished to God he could, but he wouldn't tell him anyway, even if he knew, which he did not. "I don't know if he is or he isn't," Eton said. "We're still looking for him."

"Good luck with that," the man said.

"You're still dodging the question. What is all this about?"

"I don't know," he said. "I presume the company just wants yours gone."

"*Pfft.* There's usually a little more to it than that. What's the deal?"

"No clue," he said.

"You mean, as boss, you're not in the know?"

"Funny," he said. "Just because I'm not telling you doesn't mean I don't know."

"Yeah, it does," he said. "I get it."

"Well, I'm not telling you, even if I do know, which just means you don't," he said, with a sneer.

"Whatever," he said. "You're full of shit anyway. I'm done talking. I've got things to do."

"Yeah, going after some of my other guys?" he asked. "So it depends on how cleanly they take care of Eton."

"He's not that easy to kill," Eton said, rolling his eyes at the ruse.

"Fine. Without answers," he said, "I'm not coming out."

Eton had his phone in his hand and turned it on and dialed Ice, leaving the line open. As soon as the call went through, he knew they were listening in and would track his phone.

"Like I said, Garret," the gunman said. "We know what we need to do for the mission. That's how it works. You know how compartmentalization works. You only get to know one rung up."

"Yeah, I don't generally work that way, and neither does Eton," he said, ensuring that Ice would figure out the gunman had him and Garret mixed up. "Bullard's good at keeping us all in the loop."

"I doubt it," he said. "He didn't keep you in the loop about how he felt about Ice, did he?"

"You're wrong. We all know how he feels about her," he said. "We also know how he feels about Levi. Bullard loves them both and never tries to disturb what they have together."

"I wonder if he can say that for everybody though."

At that, Eton perked up. "Is that what this is? Something personal?"

"No clue," he said. "Just doing what I'm paid to do. Paid very well, I might add."

"And you think that's all there is to it?"

At his words, Sammy turned to glare at the gunman.

"You people killed my father," she said. "You burned my home to the ground. You shot Karl. You threatened and intimidated a nice old man into betraying his values. Then you killed his son. Jesus. All that for what? Because you got paid?"

Her outrage was palpable in the air. The man just looked at her and sneered, giving her a shake. "You shut the fuck up, or I'll knock you silly."

And in a move that absolutely shocked Eton, making him wish he had just one second of warning, Sammy turned around and belted the gunman hard across the face. Eton jumped into the fray immediately and tried to grab the gun away from the guy. Meanwhile, Sammy turned and pounded her knee into the gunman's groin. The shocked gunman, now fighting off the two of them, slammed his elbow into her face, knocking her back a good six or eight feet; then she stumbled to the ground. Eton called out, "You okay?"

"Hell no, I'm not okay," she said, "but I will be. Just make sure you get that asshole."

But it wasn't an easy fight. This guy had the upper hand with a weapon, so Eton was outmatched and had to keep focused on that. Eton took a hard left before getting his right in with a heavy uppercut. That caught the guy under the jaw, snapping his head backward. He stood suspended in the air momentarily, before he collapsed to the ground.

Sammy got up and stood beside Eton. "Is he dead?"

"Possibly," he said, sure he'd heard the snap of the guy's neck. He dropped down beside the man, securing the gun and checking for a pulse. "He's alive," he said, "but I'm not sure for how long."

"Was that sound his neck breaking?"

"Maybe, but that doesn't mean it'll kill him," he said.

He quickly pocketed the gun and stepped closer, pulled out the guy's ID. He laid everything out, grabbed his phone, and took several photos. "I've never heard of this guy," he said.

"But isn't this leading to the same place you often wondered about?"

"Sure, but it appears to be layers upon layers. It looks like we won't know the end game until we run out of layers."

"It's all bullshit," she said.

Just then, weird sounds rattled up the man's chest. They both froze and looked at him, as air escaped from his throat.

"Is that what they call a death rattle?" She gasped, her hand over her mouth in horror.

"Quite possibly," he said. He quickly put the wallet back together and replaced it in the guy's pocket and then leaned forward to check for breathing. He looked at her and nodded. "He's dead." He grabbed his phone again and called Ice back. "Sorry, I lost you in the midst of the fight. Did you get all that?"

"We've got your location," she said. "I presume you're good, for the moment at least?"

"The gunman's dead," he said. "I think I broke his neck."

"Of course you did," she said drily. "Have you got a place to hide out?"

"I can't," he said, "I have to go after Garret. They've got their team coming after him."

"I'm not all that impressed with their intel, if they can't tell you two apart. Have you got wheels?"

"Our dead guy's got to have some somewhere." He turned to look at Sammy. "Where did he come from?"

She pointed down by her house.

"We'll go to her house, see if there's a car we can use,

and then we're heading after Garret."

"I want you to keep this line available for me to call back," Ice told Eton.

"Make sure you get a tracker on Garret."

"We're on it," she hung up.

The minute he hung up, something soft landed against his chest, and he wrapped his arms around her tight. "I'm so sorry," he whispered. She shook her head, without words at the moment, and just burrowed in deeper. He held her close for a long moment. "As much as I want to stay here," he said, "I can't. We have to go after Garret."

"As long as it's *we*," she whispered.

He grabbed her hand and said, "Come on. *We* have to get down there fast."

They raced down the hillside, loving the fact that she was as fit and as strong as he was. By the time they got to the base, she said, "We should have grabbed his keys."

"I did," he said, holding them up, wincing at the sight of the still-burning house.

There at the bottom, tucked around the corner, well away from the heat of the fire, was a small truck. He quickly unlocked it, letting her into her side, and said, "Let's go."

"How can you guys locate Garret?"

"Satellite technology. He's ahead of us somewhere," he said. "So we'll get in contact with Ice again and see what she's got from tracking him."

"And will she deal with that body up there?"

"Yes," he said, "at least she'll tell the police that the gunman set fire to the house, then ran up the hill and into the woods."

"Then they'll presume that he fell and broke his neck."

"Works for me," he said.

"In a way it does for me to," she said. "I just—he took so much from me."

"I know, and I'm so sorry."

CHAPTER 13

S AMMY SMILED AT Eton, but it was a teary smile. "It's not your fault," she said gently.

He looked at her and said, "If I hadn't spent time with you," he said, "you wouldn't have become a target."

"It's hard to say," she said. "You can't be sure of that."

"Pretty sure."

"Well, just like I have to walk away from it, so do you," she said, "because that's not something we can have between us."

He gave her a hard questioning look. "Are you serious?"

"Absolutely," she nodded. "This requires honesty from both of us," she said.

"And where are we going?" he asked humorously.

"I don't think it matters now," she said. "I don't have any plans. And I don't have any family left." She glanced back at her house, the fire still burning. In the distance she heard sirens coming. "They won't save anything, will they?"

"No," he said, "and it's probably just as well. There's nothing salvageable anyway at this point."

"Will there be enough of my father left to bury?"

"Yes," he said, "there will."

"And who gets to tell the story?"

"We'll let Ice handle it," he said. "She's running point on several things going on in our world right now." He quickly explained about her heading up the search for Bullard and her unusual hidden weapon, Terk, the secret operative with a psychic intuition running a team of similar men in the black ops world.

"I need an Ice in my life," she said. "That's seriously wild."

"I know, right? Unfortunately we still have no word on our missing friend, although not for the lack of trying," he said, with sincerity. "We have men back at the main compound of Bullard's camp," he said, "but we're trying to maintain radio silence to make sure we don't lead anybody back there."

"Do you know for sure," she said, "that the camp is okay?"

"Yeah, the rest of the team is keeping them in the loop."

"How many on the team?"

"Normally, boots on the ground, we're eight men out. Bullard is our eighth man in this case," he said, "and we still don't have any update on him."

"And what about the other team members?"

"Cain is running our command center until he heals up. Garret and I are out in the field. Some are checking throughout Africa and other leads. Others are checking the coastline for Bullard. They're doing the legwork. We're right in the action center though."

"Who was on the plane with Garret and Bullard?"

"Ryland," Eton said. "He was busted up pretty badly and is still recovering. At the moment, his office is out on a sailboat in the middle of the ocean. So he's enjoying life a whole lot more than he used to. Still working though."

"Sounds good to me," she said, with a smile.

He glanced at her. "Do you like sailing?"

"I wouldn't know," she said. "I've spent the bulk of my life right here."

"Are you ready for more?"

"Yes," she said. "I'm ready for a whole lot more."

"Great," he said. "It's a big world out there."

"You ready to show it to me?"

"As soon as we're done with this shit, and I'm sure that you're safe," he said, "but I won't take you anywhere before that."

"In that case," she said, snatching up his phone, "how do we get ahold of Ice?"

He chuckled. "Push that button right there," and he pointed. The call connected quickly, and a woman's voice answered.

"Hi, my name is Sammy. Eton is right here beside me."

"Hi, Sammy," Ice said in a warm voice. "We've located Garret."

"Good," Eton said into the phone, after Sammy put it on Speakerphone. "Where are we heading?"

"Only one mile away from you," she said. "You'll have to hide Sammy somewhere and make sure that you go cross-country." He followed the instructions and before long, pulled off on the side of the road. He turned and looked at her.

She smiled, nodded, and said, "I know you've got to go. I'll stay here." She handed the phone to him, after Sammy gave Ice her phone number.

"Good," Ice said. "I'll keep you in the loop."

And, with that, Eton leaned across, and, grabbing her chin, he kissed her hard and said, "Remember that," and then he was gone.

She sat in the vehicle in the darkness, wondering how

her life had gotten to this point. She knew the future was uncertain but, at the moment, felt a hell of a lot better than she had just moments earlier. She sank back into the seat, slouching down so no one driving by saw her, and settled in to wait. And waiting had to be the worst thing.

When Ice contacted her a little bit later, she said, "No news, I'm just checking in."

"Okay, I'm slouched down in the seat," she said, "and locked inside."

"Good, Garret is surrounded, and Eton has just arrived."

"He's tired and sore already, so I'm hoping he's okay for this."

"He'll be fine. Unless you think you can do anything to help," Ice said.

"Funny you would ask that," she said, "because, as far as Eton is concerned, I'm not allowed to leave this truck."

"No? But they're quite surrounded," she said. "Can you check underneath the front seat and see if there are any weapons?"

"Yes, there's a handgun," she said, pulling it out ginger-ly.

"You know how to use it?"

"In some form or fashion, yes. I used to shoot with my father, just for target practice, but I haven't held a gun for a long time."

"That's fine," she said. "I can't guarantee you won't get taken if you go up there, but what I can tell you is they need to have the odds evened up."

"Tell me where to go," she said, opening the truck door and getting out. "I'm outside."

"Head up to the hill on your right," she said.

"What is it you want me to do when I get up there?" she

asked quietly.

"We'll figure that out when you get there."

"Says you," she muttered.

Ice chuckled. "Even if it's only as a diversionary tactic," she said, "it would still help."

"Okay," she said. As she arrived in the area, she stopped and slipped behind one of the largest of the trees, following Ice's instruction. "I'm here. So now what?"

"They should be just ahead, so give yourself a minute to listen and to get oriented."

She heard voices. "Uh-oh," she said.

"Yeah, do you see a stick or a rock? Anything that you can pick up?"

"Potentially, why?"

"We want them to think that more people are out there."

"What good will that do?"

"It will throw them off, making them nervous, and they'll begin to doubt their intel," she said. "We want them to worry about who is out there. Who did they miss? Because if they missed one, chances are they missed more."

"Got it," she said. "Rocks are here and a couple sticks."

"Pick up a couple rocks that you can load your pockets down with, then get back into position," she said.

"I can almost see the area up ahead," she said.

"Okay, listen," she said. "What I want you to do, if you can, is to chuck a rock in the farthest direction. Hopefully, it will make them think somebody is coming up on them."

She did that, and instantly the voices stopped.

"But won't somebody come looking for me?"

"Nope, they'll go look for that rock. That's where the sound came from," Ice said.

That made sense. But, at the same time, it was a little bit unnerving. Sammy looked at the tree and said, "I'll go up this tree," she said, "so I'm out of the line of fire."

"Good idea," Ice said, "and I'll hang up, so I can go deal with the satellite. Stay out of sight."

"Will do." She pocketed her phone and scrambled up the tree, until she was out of sight. But she could just about see them down below. She might not have been a great shot when she was learning about guns with her dad, but she'd been a hell of a baseball player.

She pulled a rock from her pocket and studied the clear sight she had down below. And she wondered. It was a hefty distance but not so bad—she thought she could make it. The trouble was, she just didn't know how accurate she would be coming from higher off the ground. Luckily the tree had a bald spot, which would allow for her to wind up. After any pitch, she had to know that her chances were good that the bad guys would come after her. But she also had a weapon, so she wasn't completely helpless.

Just then she watched Garret being shoved into the center of the circle with a gun on him. She realized things had gotten more than serious. She picked up that rock and leaned forward. Seeing she had a clear shot, she kissed the rock, wound up for her throw, and whispered, "For Dad." Then she threw it as hard as she could.

Smack.

The rock hit the gunman square in the forehead. He stumbled. Garret spun around and grabbed the gun, then shot him, as all hell broke loose. She ducked back under cover, unsure of what to do, so she just waited, hoping the answer would present itself. But, at the moment, still just chaos. Suddenly the gunfire stopped. She wanted to call out but knew likely somebody still hid, just like she had. She sat tight against the tree. Another shot was fired, followed by three more. Then silence. Finally, just when she thought it was safe, she heard rustling below.

"Whoever the hell's here," he called out, "we've got one injured on your team." He pushed Eton forward, and she saw through the foliage that he was hurt. Blood streamed down his chest, and it look like another wound of some sort was on his head. She glared at the asshole, as he moved underneath the tree and kept looking up at the hillside, waving the gun around. "Did you hear me?" he shouted. "If you don't fucking show yourself, I'll shoot him dead right here and now."

No sign of Garret.

Eton called out, "I'm fine."

"Not now you aren't," he said. The guy cocked the handgun and put it up against his shoulder. "Don't you fucking move," he said.

She studied the two of them. And then, with an almost a fatalistic thought, she just let herself drop right onto the back of the gunman. He went down with surprise but quickly threw Sammy off him. Immediately Eton kicked the gun away, snatched it up, and shot him. Sammy looked at Eton in shock, then bounced to her feet and raced over to him.

He opened his arms and held her close.

"How badly are you hurt?"

"The blood on my chest isn't mine," he said. "I have a hell of a headache, but it's not all bad."

"What about Garret?"

"Garret's here," Garret said, as he stepped out of the trees. "Good thing I saw you make that move. I was just about ready to shoot the guy in the head."

"Glad to hear it," she said. "Is that it now? Are we done?"

The gunman on the ground at her feet made a half gurgling sound. "It's not over," he said, coughing. "It's just one more layer."

Garret leaned over and asked, "Who's behind this?"

"You'll find out," he said. "Don't worry. You'll find out."

And, with that, he died.

ETON HELD SAMMY tight against his chest. "Remember that part about staying in the vehicle?"

"Yeah, well, lucky for me and for you," she said, "Ice doesn't believe in keeping the little woman safe."

At that, he chuckled. "No, that's very true," he said. "She won't love me right now." He pulled out his phone and called Ice and said, "Well, I won't thank you for sending Sammy here in the middle of the gunfight."

Sammy leaned into the phone. "But he'll thank you anyway because I saved his ass," she said, with a smirk.

"Is all well that ends well?" Ice asked, her voice hard, "Details, please."

He quickly filled her in on what happened. "You've got six bodies up here now."

"Great," she said. "Are you prepared to leave Switzerland, because, after the last phone call I made to the powers that be, they wanted you out of there before more chaos hit. I can only imagine what they'll say this time."

"Well, I'm ready to leave," he said, "but I'm bringing Sammy with me."

"And he's hurt," Sammy said. "We need a place for him

to hole up for a couple days and heal."

"Good," Ice said, "as long as it's not too bad of an injury?"

"No," he said, "a head injury. I just need to relax a minute."

Garret giggled like a schoolgirl and said, "He definitely needs a couple days in bed." No doubting the innuendo within his tone.

Sammy just glared at him. "Very funny. What are you, fourteen?"

He smirked and said to Ice, "Send them off someplace when they're good to go. Me, I'm heading back to the team," he said. "We need to regroup. A lot of shit came out of this mess, but I don't know that we have any decent answers yet."

"We have more than I expected," Ice said. "And not all of it is bad. So, yes, we'll have you head home to regroup, and we'll start Eton and Sammy driving. We'll find you two a spot to hole up in. Just give me a few minutes." And, just like that, she hung up.

Eton sighed, looking sleepy, and said, "You're not wrong about needing a couple days in bed."

Moments later, Ice called. "We've got a place for you," she said. "About a forty-five-minute drive. Can you make it?"

"He can make it," Garret said. "I'll drive." And it was arranged just that fast. Less than an hour later, they pulled into the hotel. Garret dropped them off and said, "Okay, I'm heading to the airport in the truck. Ice has a new vehicle for you coming soon. I'll fill you in as soon as I get back home." He gave Eton a slap on the shoulder. "You make sure you stay here until you're healed."

"I'm not going anywhere for a bit," Eton said, and, indeed, he was fading quickly.

Garret studied him for a long moment and said, "Yeah, don't be a fool. You were pissed off at me for coming back too early," he said, "so let's make sure that you don't follow the same pattern."

"We'll see if that's an option," he said, "but I hear you. Now go catch your plane," Eton said. The two men shook hands, then, after a hug for Sammy, Garret was gone. Minutes later they walked into the hotel room. Eton took one look at the bed and groaned. "I just want to be horizontal."

"Shower first," she said. "You'll feel better."

He stripped off his clothes with her help, but, as they pulled off his shirt, more injuries were revealed.

She stared at him. "Oh, my God."

"Don't freak out," he said. "I'm fine."

She shook her head. "You're not fine at all, but it looks like you will be."

"Exactly." He stripped down completely nude and stepped into the shower.

CHAPTER 14

S AMMY STOOD THERE, with his dirty clothes, wondering what she should do. They didn't have any extra clothing or anything else, even a hairbrush. A knock came at the door, just as she got a phone call from Ice. "Arriving at your door is their stuff from the chalet," she said. "Order some food in whenever you're ready, and you guys can hole up for a couple days. Don't move without letting us know."

"We won't be moving. He's more injured than I realized," Sammy said. "Not badly, just more scrapes, scratches, and bruising."

"Those are minor," she said. "Nothing worse than that? No bullet wounds besides the graze to his head?"

"Not that I've seen, no."

"Then you're good to go," she said, and, with that, Ice hung up.

Sammy opened the door to see nobody outside, but the bags were there. She brought them in and realized that her purse was there as well as whatever the guys had left at the chalet, plus some toiletries for her. She walked into the bathroom and said, "We've got a change of clothes for you here."

"Good," he said. "I could use it."

She stepped back out again and realized how late it was. So much had happened that she hadn't had a chance to sort out any of it yet. Then she sat on the bed, thinking about her father. She could feel the tears coming on. She let herself cry, really cry over her loss, until she felt his arms wrapped around her shoulders. She snuggled in close and said, "I'm fine."

"Yeah, me too," he said, with a note of humor.

She tilted her head and looked up at him, tears clinging to the tips of her eyelashes, and smiled. "I'll miss him terribly."

"Of course you will," he said, "and the life you shared with him there."

"True, but I can make another life," she said.

He leaned down and kissed her hard. "That's what I'm counting on."

"I sure didn't expect a new life to happen this way," she said.

"We never do," he murmured. He pulled back the blankets and said, "I don't know about you, but I need some sleep."

"If I could sleep, it'd be great," she admitted. "It's been a rough day."

"It's been a rough couple days," he said, as he flipped back the sheet and patted the side of the bed. "Left side or right for you?"

"Whichever you don't want," she said. "I'm easy." She went into the bathroom and scrubbed her face, thought about a shower and quickly stripped down. She climbed into the shower, realizing she'd picked up a few scrapes and bruises herself. After a five-minute shower, she was too tired for anything more. She dried off and crawled into bed beside him, to find he was already out cold. She snuggled up and let his body heat wrap around her.

"Tomorrow's a new day," he whispered, pulling her close. "Let's sleep this one away."

She closed her eyes and slept.

ETON WOKE UP, his body sore and achy, but something warm that smelled delicious was in his arms. He smiled.

"What are you smiling at?" she murmured.

"How do you know I'm smiling?" He tucked her up close, loving the feel of her skin against his. There was something so intimate and yet so natural about it.

"I can feel it," she said. She leaned up and kissed him on the cheek. "I don't think it's morning. Looks like we skipped that part of the day."

He rolled over and checked his clock. "It's two o'clock in the afternoon," he said. "Wow."

"That's what I mean."

"Have you been awake long?"

"Somewhere around the time you smiled," she murmured, burrowing in deeper.

He chuckled. "In other words, you haven't been asleep very long."

"Awake, you mean. Jeez, did you get hit on the head or what?"

He tilted her chin and kissed her, then hopped up and walked to the bathroom. When he returned, he slipped back under the blankets.

Then she raced to the bathroom and came right back as well. As she did, she said, "It's a rainy day out there."

"I didn't really want to spend any time outside anyway," he said.

She looked at him, "How is the head?"

"Feels like it got kicked around a bit."

"Looks a little like it too," she said, with a smile.

"Hey, did I mention how you look after getting punched in the face yesterday?"

"Oh, hush."

He flung the blankets back and said, "Were you anxious to leave the bed, or are you getting back in?"

Standing there completely nude, she looked at herself and smiled. "Nope. I wasn't planning on leaving it for the rest of the day. Although we will need food at some point."

"Right," he said, "not sure what we should do about that. Are you hungry, hungry like need it now?"

"No, not now, but soon," she murmured. He picked up his phone and sent a message to his team. "Don't tell me that they'll order food for you?"

"Absolutely," he said. "If anybody's nearby, they'll deliver it too. But, in the meantime, they'll set it up, so it's ordered and won't be tracked back to us."

"Perfect." She slipped back under the covers and said, "How long?"

"I told them an hour."

"Oh, good." She snuggled under the blankets and closed her eyes.

"Did you have something you wanted to do for the next hour?" he asked, as he nuzzled her neck.

She smiled, wrapped an arm around him, and then flipped over, so she faced him. "I'm sure we can find something," she said. He leaned down and first kissed her gently, then a little harder, then harder yet again. She sighed happily, stretched out along his lean length, wrapping her leg around his hip and thigh. "I didn't really expect to find somebody through this nightmare," she said. "My father's one wish for me was that I would be settled before he passed on."

"Well, he might not know about it, but I'm pretty sure you're settled," he murmured against her lips.

"Am I though?" she asked, her gaze twinkling up at him.

"Oh, you are," he said, and, leaning over, he kissed her hard. She wrapped her arms around him and hung on tight, and he could feel the heat building between them. He was loving every second of it. She opened her eyes, looked up at him and whispered, "Thank you."

He raised one eyebrow. "Thank you?"

"For saving my life."

"We got your home burned down with your dad's body in it. I'm so sorry about that. It must have been awful for you."

"Not your fault," she said. "And, if we hadn't had that warning, Garret and I may have gotten picked off, trying to get out, if not consumed by the fire. And, if I'd been asleep, I wouldn't have gotten out of the house at all, and, with my last thoughts, I wouldn't have known about Dad."

He kissed her again. "I don't even want to think about it," he said. "I'll have nightmares about this one for a long time."

"I know," she said, "a lot of close calls. At least we have this moment. And each other."

He said, "I'm sorry that I never had a chance to meet your father, but I'm grateful to him for leaving such a wonderful daughter behind."

She smiled. "You say the nicest things."

"Because I mean them," he said sincerely.

She smiled and said, "And you can look after me, huh?"

He chuckled. "Is that part of the deal?"

"Only as far as he's concerned," she said. "I prefer Ice's take, and, when shit's about to fly down the pipeline, I need to be just as prepared as you."

He rolled his eyes at that. "Nobody in this world would get away with telling Ice that she should stay in the vehicle," he said.

"She didn't want to lose you two up there, and neither did I."

"The good thing is, you didn't," he said, with a smile, "and now we have a few days just to ourselves."

"Perfect," she said and opened her arms.

CHAPTER 15

S AMMY COULDN'T BELIEVE how swollen her heart felt right now. It overflowed with joy, love, sorrow, grief, surprise, and adventure. Her emotions were so overwhelming and so deep that she couldn't sort them out and had no intention of trying to right now. "I suggest we enjoy every moment of time we have," she murmured. When she wrapped her arms around his neck and said, "Especially this way."

And he kissed her, their mouths and their tongues warring gently as they eased into it, but passion struck hard and fast, and before long, she twisted beneath him, pleading with him to put her out of her misery. He rose above her, his hands holding her arms high above her head, and entered in one full plunge. She groaned, settled, and shifted, as he paused for a moment, and, still holding her arms, her legs high up around his hips, he lifted up. He groaned and started to move rapidly, until they both cried out in joy. When he finally collapsed beside her, she whispered, "This is a great way to spend a few days."

He chuckled. "I hear you," he said. "I need to heal up a bit to get back to full strength."

"Did that hurt your head?"

"Absolutely no way," he said.

"Perfect," she said. "We can keep doing this all day

then."

He chuckled. "Maybe not all day," he murmured. "But I'm totally okay to see how much we can get through over the next couple days."

"No contest," she said, "just a gentle, enjoyable time for the two of us."

"Perfect," he said, then checked the time. "By the way, we're coming up on an hour."

"Perfect," she said. "I need food." She got out of bed and walked over to his bag. "So, do you want any clothes?"

"No, just my boxers," he said, which she tossed to him, and he put on. "And that's only because I need to answer the door."

She smiled and asked, "Can I have the T-shirt then?"

He looked over just as she put his T-shirt over her head. "I like it better on you anyway," he joked.

She smiled, as it just went down to the top of her thighs.

When she heard an odd knock at the door, he walked over, then waited while it was repeated. He counted down from five to one. And at one, he opened the door. She came up to his side and looked around the hallway, but nobody was there. Two large bags of food were on the ground outside their room. He picked them up, brought them inside. "Well, we won't starve."

"Oh, I am loving this," she said. "Seriously, we won't have any interruptions?"

"No, no interruptions."

"And Garret is safe?"

"Garret is safe," he said.

She frowned, looked at him, and said, "You are sure about that, right?"

"He texted me earlier this morning to say that he'd landed safely in Australia."

"Good," she said, "because I don't trust him to stay put."

"I said he was safe. I didn't say anything about him staying put."

"Do you think he's in danger?"

"Absolutely he's in danger," he said quietly. "And, if I know Garret, he's had about enough of the guy who hired these assholes."

"And what about us?" she asked. "What are we supposed to do?"

"We're here for three days," he said, "And then … how do you feel about traveling to Australia?"

Her gaze widened. "I've never been."

"And?"

She smiled. "I'd be delighted to go."

"Do you have a passport?"

She nodded. "I have all my papers, thanks to Garret. I just don't have any clothes."

"Personally I think what you're wearing is perfect," he said, "or you could always wear Garret's. His bag is over there. Or I can put in an order for a few things, when I have them arrange for the tickets so we can get home."

"Is Australia home?"

"No, but it's one of the bases we were looking at setting up," he said. "Africa is home."

"Africa?" she said, surprised.

He smiled and said, "Yeah, don't worry. You'll love it."

She smiled, wrapped her arms around him, and said, "I'm sure I will. As long as you're there."

"Not sure about needing any architects there though," he murmured.

"I have a lot of clients all over the world," she said. "Not to worry. I'll keep busy wherever I am."

"And, if you don't," he said, tilting her head up and giving her a long deep soul-searching kiss. "I've got ideas on how to fill your time."

She laughed. "I like the sound of that just fine."

EPILOGUE

G ARRET BALDERSON LANDED in Perth and walked out of the airport to see Kano standing there, waiting for him. "Any news?"

"On Bullard, no," Kano said. "On the guys who hired the men you just took out, yes. Come on. Let's get going."

"Will we be centered in Australia?"

"No," Kano said. "Sounds like we're heading to England."

"England, huh? Why am I not surprised? Have you done a full rundown on Kingdom Securities?"

"Yeah, and some questions have definitely come up."

"Okay, so now what?" asked Garret.

"Let's talk," Kano said.

"I'll talk, providing you've got a direction for me to go."

"We do," Kano said. "I just want you to calm down. Hold your horses a little, and let's get a play in place."

"Absolutely," Garret said. "Let's do it."

"Did you hear from Eton?" Kano asked.

"He's fine, healing up. The two of them are doing great, and they'll be in Australia in three days."

"Good," Kano said.

"I can't believe that's three for three," Garret said. "Wait 'til you see Sammy."

"A looker, is she? Does she have heart?"

"More than we've seen from a lot of people," he said, explaining how the last craziness up on the hilltop went down and her role in it.

Kano chuckled. "Right in the forehead? While perched in a tree? Come on. You're making that up."

"I'm not though. That's the thing," Garret replied.

"Well," Kano said, "you've got to love a woman who can throw a pitch like that."

"Exactly. Kano, come on. What is it you're holding back?"

"Let me explain," he said. "We just don't have all the answers we need yet."

"We have to have something," Garret said.

"There was a woman," Kano said, "one not all that unknown to us."

"Who? What are you talking about?"

"She may have intel on Kingdom Securities."

"Who is she?"

Kano took a deep breath and said, "You know her."

"I know a lot of women, Kano. I'm just that kind of guy," he said, with a ridiculous grin. "What about her?"

"That's who you'll meet up with in England."

"Why?"

"She has information," he said.

"Information on …? Come on. What?"

"On your brother." The words came out in a rush, and Kano looked like he wanted to disappear.

Garret stared at him in shock. "What are you talking about?"

"Your brother has been working for Kingdom."

"No, he hasn't. Why would Gregg do that? It makes no sense."

"Yes, he has," he said. "And she has information on it."

"No way. And I care about her intel, why?"

"She implied, whether it's right or wrong, that your brother might have had something to do with the attack on you and Bullard."

"Are you saying that it wasn't Bullard they were trying to take out, but it was me?"

The words were like a stab to the heart. He'd been so focused on who was trying to take out Bullard that it never occurred to him that it might have been personal against someone else, least of all him.

"That's what we're considering," he said.

"Why would my brother do that?"

"I don't know," Kano said. "You tell me."

"There's no reason for it, no motive," he said. "My brother and I have always been close."

"Are you sure?"

"Yes, I'm sure," he said. "It makes no sense."

"Well, Amy is over there, and she's willing to talk."

He groaned. "Amy? Jesus, that's all I need."

"Yeah," Kano said.

Garret looked at him. "You know she was my girlfriend, right? My fiancée?"

Kano nodded slowly. "I know."

"And you know she cheated on me with my brother, right?"

Kano winced. "I heard rumors, yes."

"And you know we can't trust anything she says, right?"

"That assumption would be implied, based on the circumstances of your relationship," Kano agreed.

"So why the hell am I wasting time going over there to listen to anything she has to say?"

"Because your brother has disappeared," he said. "And that's something I'm pretty sure you'll want to deal with."

"Shit," he said. "When am I leaving?"

"You see that I haven't turned on the engine, right?"

He looked at him, back at the airport, and said, "Now?"

"You're flying out in an hour and twenty," he said. "I brought your extra gear bag. Eton will bring back your stuff from the chalet with him."

"Who's coming with me?"

"I am," Kano said. "This time I'll be your backup."

Garret said, "Let's do it then."

This concludes Book 3 of Bullard's Battle: Eton's Escape.
Read about Garret's Gambit: Bullard's Battle, Book 4

Garret's Gambit: Bullard's Battle (Book #4)

Welcome to a new stand-alone but interconnected series from Dale Mayer. This is Bullard's story—and that of his team's. All raw, rough, incredibly capable men who have one goal: to find out who was behind the attack on their leader, before the attacker, or attackers, return to finish the job.

Stay tuned for more nonstop action as the men narrow down their suspects ... and find a way to let love back into their own empty lives.

Stronger than he had any right to be after the plane explosion and still angry about it all, Garret's seriously unimpressed to fly to London to speak with an ex-fiancée who'd screwed him over with his own brother. But she had information on his missing brother, who was a link to the plane crash that sent Garret into the ocean.

Yet Astra, not Amy, waits in London for Garret, to explain the little she knows, hoping he'll let go of some of his resentment and help her look for her sister, Amy—who disappears just before Garret's arrival. Some coincidence there. Then her sister hasn't faced the music for any of her actions in a long time. Today is no different. Too bad Amy and Garret hadn't broken up much earlier. It might have given Astra a chance with the man she has loved since forever.

Still, if finding Astra's sister leads Garret to finding his brother, who might be able to give them answers regarding the sabotaged plane, then Astra's happy to play the game. However, it's not that easy, as the men who failed to kill the two team members are still looking for their chance to finish the job. And to take out anyone who is close by ...

Find Book 4 here!

To find out more visit Dale Mayer's website.

smarturl.it/DMSGarret

Damon's Deal: Terkel's Team (Book #1)

Welcome to a brand-new connected series of intrigue, betrayal, and ... murder, from the *USA Today* best-selling author Dale Mayer. A series with all the elements you've come to love, plus so much more... including psychics!

A betrayal from within has Terkel frantic to protect those he can, as his team falls one by one, from a murderous killer he helped create.

ICE POURED HERSELF a coffee and sat down at the compound's massive dining room table with the others. When her phone rang, she smiled at the number displayed. "Hey, Terk. How're you doing?" She put the call on Speakerphone.

"I'm okay," Terkel said, his voice distracted and tight.

"Terk?" Merk called from across the table. He got up and walked closer and sat across from Levi. "You don't sound too good, brother. What's up?"

"I'm fine," Terk said. "Or I will be. Right now, things are blown to shit."

"As in literally?" Merk asked.

"The entire group," Terk said, "they're all gone. I had a solid team of eight, and they're all gone."

"Dead?"

Several others stood to join them, gathered around Ice's phone. Levi stepped forward, his hand on Ice's shoulder. "Terk? Are they all dead?"

"No." Terk took a deep breath. "I'm not making sense. I'm sorry."

"Take it easy," Ice said, her voice calm and reassuring. "What do you mean, *they're all gone*?"

"All their abilities are gone," he said. "Something's happened to them. Somebody has deliberately removed whatever super senses they could utilize—or what we have been utilizing for the last ten years for the government." His tone was bitter. "When the US gov recently closed us down, they promised that our black ops department would never rise again, but I didn't expect them to attack us personally."

"What are you talking about?" Merk said in alarm, standing up now to stare at Ice's phone. "Are you in danger?"

"Maybe? I don't know," Terk said. "I need to find out exactly what the hell's going on."

"What can we do to help?" Ice asked.

Terk gave a broken laugh. "That's not why I'm calling. Well, it is, but it isn't."

Ice looked at Merk, who frowned, as he shook his head. Ice knew he and the others had heard Terk's stressed out tone and the completely confusing bits and pieces coming from his mouth. Ice said, "Terk, you're not making sense again. Take a breath and explain. Please. You're scaring me."

Terk took a long slow deep breath. "Tell Stone to open the gate," he said. "She's out there."

"Who's out there?" Levi asked, hopped up, looked outside, and shrugged.

"She's coming up the road now. You have to let her in."

"Who? Why?"

"*Because*," he said, "she's also harnessed with C-4."

"Jesus," Levi said, bolting to display the camera feeds to the big screen in the room. "Is it live?"

"It is, and she's been sent to you."

"Well, that's an interesting move," Ice said, her voice sharp, activating her comm to connect to Stone in the control room. "Who's after us?"

"I think it's rebels within the Iranian government. But it could be our own government. I don't know anymore," Terk snapped. "I also don't know how they got her so close to you. Or how they pinned your connection to me," he said. "I've been very careful."

"We can look after ourselves," Ice said immediately. "But who is this woman to you?"

"She's pregnant," he said, "so that adds to the intensity here."

"Understood. So who is the father? Is he connected somehow?"

There was silence on the other end.

Merk said, "Terk, talk to us."

"She's carrying my baby," Terk replied, his voice heavy.

Merk, his expression grim, looked at Ice, her face mirroring his shock. He asked, "How do you know her, Terk?"

"Brother, you don't understand," Terk said. "I've never met this woman before in my life." And, with that, the phone went dead.

Find Book 1 here!

To find out more visit Dale Mayer's website.

smarturl.it/DMSTTDamon

Author's Note

Thank you for reading Eton's Escape: Bullard's Battle, Book 3! If you enjoyed the book, please take a moment and leave a short review.

Dear reader,

I love to hear from readers, and you can contact me at my website: www.dalemayer.com or at my Facebook author page. To be informed of new releases and special offers, sign up for my newsletter or follow me on BookBub. And if you are interested in joining Dale Mayer's Reader Group, here is the Facebook sign up page.
https://smarturl.it/DaleMayerFBGroup

Cheers,
Dale Mayer

Get THREE Free Books Now!

Have you met the SEALS of Honor?

SEALs of Honor Books 1, 2, and 3. Follow the stories of brave, badass warriors who serve their country with honor and love their women to the limits of life and death.

Read Mason, Hawk, and Dane right now for FREE.

Go here and tell me where to send them!
http://smarturl.it/EthanBofB

About the Author

Dale Mayer is a *USA Today* best-selling author, best known for her SEALs military romances, her Psychic Visions series, and her Lovely Lethal Garden cozy series. Her contemporary romances are raw and full of passion and emotion (Broken But ... Mending series). Her thrillers will keep you guessing (By Death series), and her romantic comedies will keep you giggling (*It's a Dog's Life*, a stand-alone novella; and the Broken Protocols series, starring Charming Marvin, the cat).

Dale honors the stories that come to her—and some of them are crazy and break all the rules and cross multiple genres!

To go with her fiction, she also writes nonfiction in many different fields, with books available on résumé writing, companion gardening, and the US mortgage system. She has recently published her Career Essentials series. All her books are available in print and ebook format.

Connect with Dale Mayer Online

Dale's Website – www.dalemayer.com
Twitter – @DaleMayer
Facebook – facebook.com/DaleMayer.author
BookBub – bookbub.com/authors/dale-mayer

Also by Dale Mayer

Published Adult Books:

Bullard's Battle
Ryland's Reach, Book 1
Cain's Cross, Book 2
Eton's Escape, Book 3
Garret's Gambit, Book 4
Kano's Keep, Book 5
Fallon's Flaw, Book 6
Quinn's Quest, Book 7
Bullard's Beauty, Book 8
Bullard's Best, Book 9

Terkel's Team
Damon's Deal, Book 1

Kate Morgan
Simon Says… Hide, Book 1

Hathaway House
Aaron, Book 1
Brock, Book 2
Cole, Book 3
Denton, Book 4

The K9 Files

Harley, Book 14

The K9 Files, Books 1–2

The K9 Files, Books 3–4

The K9 Files, Books 5–6

The K9 Files, Books 7–8

The K9 Files, Books 9–10

The K9 Files, Books 11–12

Lovely Lethal Gardens

Arsenic in the Azaleas, Book 1

Bones in the Begonias, Book 2

Corpse in the Carnations, Book 3

Daggers in the Dahlias, Book 4

Evidence in the Echinacea, Book 5

Footprints in the Ferns, Book 6

Gun in the Gardenias, Book 7

Handcuffs in the Heather, Book 8

Ice Pick in the Ivy, Book 9

Jewels in the Juniper, Book 10

Killer in the Kiwis, Book 11

Lifeless in the Lilies, Book 12

Murder in the Marigolds, Book 13

Lovely Lethal Gardens, Books 1–2

Lovely Lethal Gardens, Books 3–4

Lovely Lethal Gardens, Books 5–6

Lovely Lethal Gardens, Books 7–8

Lovely Lethal Gardens, Books 9–10

Psychic Vision Series

Tuesday's Child

Hide 'n Go Seek

Maddy's Floor

Garden of Sorrow

Knock Knock...

Rare Find

Eyes to the Soul

Now You See Her

Shattered

Into the Abyss

Seeds of Malice

Eye of the Falcon

Itsy-Bitsy Spider

Unmasked

Deep Beneath

From the Ashes

Stroke of Death

Ice Maiden

Snap, Crackle...

Psychic Visions Books 1–3

Psychic Visions Books 4–6

Psychic Visions Books 7–9

By Death Series

Touched by Death

Haunted by Death

Chilled by Death

By Death Books 1–3

Broken Protocols – Romantic Comedy Series

Cat's Meow

Cat's Pajamas

Cat's Cradle

Cat's Claus

Broken Protocols 1-4

Broken and... Mending

Skin

Scars

Scales (of Justice)

Broken but... Mending 1-3

Glory

Genesis

Tori

Celeste

Glory Trilogy

Biker Blues

Morgan: Biker Blues, Volume 1

Cash: Biker Blues, Volume 2

SEALs of Honor

Mason: SEALs of Honor, Book 1

Hawk: SEALs of Honor, Book 2

Dane: SEALs of Honor, Book 3

Swede: SEALs of Honor, Book 4

Shadow: SEALs of Honor, Book 5

Cooper: SEALs of Honor, Book 6

Heroes for Hire

Levi's Legend: Heroes for Hire, Book 1

Stone's Surrender: Heroes for Hire, Book 2

Merk's Mistake: Heroes for Hire, Book 3

Rhodes's Reward: Heroes for Hire, Book 4

Flynn's Firecracker: Heroes for Hire, Book 5

Logan's Light: Heroes for Hire, Book 6

Harrison's Heart: Heroes for Hire, Book 7

Saul's Sweetheart: Heroes for Hire, Book 8

Dakota's Delight: Heroes for Hire, Book 9

Michael's Mercy (Part of Sleeper SEAL Series)

Tyson's Treasure: Heroes for Hire, Book 10

Jace's Jewel: Heroes for Hire, Book 11

Rory's Rose: Heroes for Hire, Book 12

Brandon's Bliss: Heroes for Hire, Book 13

Liam's Lily: Heroes for Hire, Book 14

North's Nikki: Heroes for Hire, Book 15

Anders's Angel: Heroes for Hire, Book 16

Reyes's Raina: Heroes for Hire, Book 17

Dezi's Diamond: Heroes for Hire, Book 18

Vince's Vixen: Heroes for Hire, Book 19

Ice's Icing: Heroes for Hire, Book 20

Johan's Joy: Heroes for Hire, Book 21

Galen's Gemma: Heroes for Hire, Book 22

Zack's Zest: Heroes for Hire, Book 23

Bonaparte's Belle: Heroes for Hire, Book 24

Noah's Nemesis: Heroes for Hire, Book 25

Heroes for Hire, Books 1–3

SEALs of Steel

The Mavericks

Gavin, Book 11

Shane, Book 12

Diesel, Book 13

Jerricho, Book 14

The Mavericks, Books 1–2

The Mavericks, Books 3–4

The Mavericks, Books 5–6

The Mavericks, Books 7–8

The Mavericks, Books 9–10

The Mavericks, Books 11–12

Collections

Dare to Be You…

Dare to Love…

Dare to be Strong…

RomanceX3

Standalone Novellas

It's a Dog's Life

Riana's Revenge

Second Chances

Published Young Adult Books:

Family Blood Ties Series

Vampire in Denial

Vampire in Distress

Vampire in Design

Vampire in Deceit

Vampire in Defiance

Vampire in Conflict

Vampire in Chaos

Vampire in Crisis

Vampire in Control

Vampire in Charge

Family Blood Ties Set 1–3

Family Blood Ties Set 1–5

Family Blood Ties Set 4–6

Family Blood Ties Set 7–9

Sian's Solution, A Family Blood Ties Series Prequel Novelette

Design series

Dangerous Designs

Deadly Designs

Darkest Designs

Design Series Trilogy

Standalone

In Cassie's Corner

Gem Stone (a Gemma Stone Mystery)

Time Thieves

Published Non-Fiction Books:

Career Essentials

Career Essentials: The Résumé

Career Essentials: The Cover Letter

Career Essentials: The Interview

Career Essentials: 3 in 1

Made in the USA
Middletown, DE
06 April 2021